Emma's Rodeo Cowboy

Shirley Penick

Shirley Penick

Photography by Wander Aquiar

Cover Models: Natasha Kirsby & Preston Thompson

Editing by Carol Tietsworth

Contact me:

www.shirleypenick.com

www.facebook.com/ShirleyPenickAuthor

To sign up for Shirley's New Release Newsletter, send email to shirleypenick@outlook.com, subject newsletter.

Dedication

To my kid's Jonathan and Sarah, because being a mom is awesome and you two support me in all that I do.

I love you!

Chapter 1

Zach McCoy dreaded the next eight seconds more than any other time in his life. Not because he was at the rodeo about to ride some bull that could possibly stomp the living shit right out of him, if he got thrown. Not because he was standing at the front of a church with his best friend who was getting married. Not because he was all dressed up in a monkey suit to be the best man. Nope, none of those things phased him. He loved the thrill of bull riding. He was happy for his best friend having found his second half. He was certainly capable of keeping Drew from passing out, and he didn't even mind that the tuxedo felt too small and confining.

Nope, what he was dreading with every part of his soul, was the five-year-old boy about to walk down the aisle as the ring bearer. He wasn't sure he could bear to see Emma's illegitimate son. Not because he was born out of wedlock, but because it meant that Emma, who he had loved from afar, since the day he moved to Spirit Lake Colorado fourteen years ago, had had sex with another man. That about killed him to even think about. It was the sole reason he hadn't been back, to what he thought of as his home town, in six long years.

Fortunately for him, his mother had relocated to Tucson to live with his sister, about the time he'd gone off to be a rodeo cowboy. A move he made six years ago—ironically enough—to keep his hands off Emma until she had graduated from high school and was old enough for him to finally make his move. They were only two years apart in age, but she was in high school and he'd graduated, so that two-year gap was a lot at seventeen and nineteen, once she graduated it would be a whole other story.

She'd been a senior in high school and so damn beautiful he'd had erotic dreams about her every night. To the point that he had to get away before he did something, that he would regret. Some of the dreams had been so vivid he'd not known how to interact with her afterward. He'd been fairly certain she'd have been onboard with joining him in those acts. They seemed to have a connection that went far beyond friendship.

So, to avoid temptation, he'd sucked it up and ridden off to join the pro-rodeo circuit, thinking it would only be a year or two before he came back and asked Emma to be his wife. But before he'd even ridden in his first professional rodeo, she'd hooked up with some drifter and had gotten pregnant. He'd felt betrayed, devastated, and furious. If he'd had one red cent to his name he'd have driven back and confronted her. But everything he had, he'd sunk into entry fees and gear.

The music changing pulled Zach out of his thoughts, and the doors opened to the chapel. He hauled in a breath and held it as he watched the small boy walk down the aisle with confidence, holding the little pillow with the rings tied on top. When he got within a few feet, Zach's breath whooshed out of him so fast, he felt gut punched.

He nearly staggered as the little boy walked up to stand next to Drew. The boy was the spitting image of himself at that age. What the fuck? Zach was shocked no one else had noticed. Of course, he hadn't moved to town until he was eleven and had started to grow into his adult height and facial features, his hair had darkened by then also.

The boy had the same dimples in his cheeks, he had the same wildly curly dark blond hair Zach had. Even had the same build he'd had at that age and he was holding the pillow in his left hand, which indicated he might be a lefty just like he was. There was no doubt about it, that boy was his son. The only difference were the chocolate brown eyes. Those were Emma's eyes.

Movement attracted his attention and Emma and some guy slipped into the end of the pew where Drew's family was sitting. Emma kept her eyes on the boy until he waved, seeing where she was so he could join her later. When she finally raised her eyes to Zach his whole being filled with that rush of love, he'd always felt around her.

Then fury burned through that love leaving him fuming with rage. He had to look away from her before he left Drew's side and went over and strangled her. How dare she keep his son from him? How dare she tell everyone it was some tourist that had gotten her pregnant? He didn't know how or when it had happened, but that was his son, no one else's. That was something he was so sure of; he would stake his life on it.

And just who in the hell was that guy with her?

Zach had to work to force himself to concentrate on the wedding procession as the bride came down the aisle, and he joined in to do his part. Emma's deception could wait until this day was over, but then she was going to have some explaining to do.

∞∞∞∞

Emma was livid, just what was with that expression she'd seen on Zach's face? Damn him, he'd been the one to turn his back on her and his son. So, what was with the attitude, like she'd somehow wronged him? He was furious. His blue eyes were ice cold and she could see the banked fury in them, but she had no idea why. Emma Kipling had never seen such a hate-filled look in her entire life. Her skin was like ice and she was shaking with anger. She didn't know what to do or what to say.

She wanted to slap that look right off his face. She'd imagined a lot of scenarios with him coming back home and seeing their son. But the cold, cruel expression she'd seen just now was not one she had ever envisioned.

Emma was damn glad she'd invited Ian to come as her date. Of course, she knew the sweet doctor would read more into it than she wanted, but there was no way she could handle seeing Zach without backup.

Dr. Ian McDonahue was new in town. He'd set up a family practice and was working hard to establish an urgent care facility. Something they could certainly use in their town. The next closest one was in Granby which was a thirty-five-minute drive. Not terrible for non-threatening emergencies, but not great either.

Dr. Ian had been looking for a bookkeeper and she'd taken him as a client. He'd asked her out on several occasions, and she'd turned him down every time, right up until her brother had announced that Zach had agreed to be his best man. Then she'd invited Ian to the wedding as a sort of shield.

She'd not known what else to do. None of her family knew Zach was Tony's father, why they had all decided she'd hooked up with some stranger she would never know. But that's what they all believed, and she'd never set them straight. Mostly because she'd been certain Zach would come home, once he heard she was pregnant. When he didn't, she'd felt confused, and betrayed, and totally embarrassed that he didn't want her and Tony.

By the time she'd realized Zach had truly abandoned her, the drifter idea was firmly in place. She'd wondered over the years if she should have contacted Zach herself, rather than leaving it up to Drew to tell his best friend, but she'd never had Zach's phone number. They'd never actually dated; it had always just been a group of them. Even the night Tony had been conceived it had been a group farewell party, until Emma had taken things into her own hands.

Her thoughts returned to the wedding in time to see Tony do his part, by offering the pillow up to the minister, who patiently untied the rings. As soon as they were off his pillow Tony ran past his father and Drew's other attendants and pushed his way into the pew to sit between her and Ian.

She'd only introduced Tony to the man a couple of days ago, and he wasn't too fond of the idea that the doctor who would be giving him his shots, was friends with his mother.

Emma smiled down at her son and ruffled his long curly hair, he was trying to look like Aquaman and had convinced her to let it grow long, Drew and Lily hadn't minded him having long hair. It was a lot curlier than she'd realized it would be. Curly hair didn't come from her side of the family, so it must be a trait from his father, as was the left-handedness. She'd never seen Zach with hair over an inch long, so the curls had been a surprise. "You did a wonderful job, Tony."

Tony grinned back up at her. "Thanks mama, but I've had a lot of practice. Four times, now."

"I guess you have." She chuckled. "Well, you did a good job in all four weddings."

He sighed and swung his legs, not quite connecting with the pew in front of them. "I hope everyone is done getting married, now."

One of the scenarios Emma had dreamt about was Zach coming back, seeing her and his child and falling to his knees to beg her forgiveness. Clearly, that wasn't happening, and she'd never felt anything for any other man, so she could reassure her son. "I'm sure we're done with weddings for a while. In fact, maybe yours will be the next one."

Tony looked so horrified at that idea she nearly laughed out loud. Instead, she turned her focus back to the ceremony taking place and tried very hard not to look at the man standing next to her brother. He looked so damn good in that tux, if he hadn't looked at her so coldly, she might have overheated seeing him looking so sexy.

Emma just wanted to get this day over so Zach would go back to the rodeo and leave her alone, but by the way he'd looked at her she was certain there would be at least one conversation between them. She hoped he would at least wait until after Drew and Lily headed off to their honeymoon. They were going to spend two nights in cabin two, where they had first been together and then on Monday they were flying off to some undisclosed location for a week.

She also hoped Zach wouldn't be cruel to Tony. He'd always been a nice guy and never deliberately cruel, but she had no idea if he'd changed in the last six years, being on the rodeo circuit. Emma really did not have any idea what to expect. She simply didn't know him any longer and couldn't count on him being the sweet boy she remembered, especially since he'd abandoned her and Tony.

Maybe he was a jerk and had always hidden it. She didn't have a clue as to what to expect. If he was mean to Tony, he would see a side of her he'd never seen either, mama bear didn't put up with much when her son was involved.

Chapter 2

The minister announced. "I now pronounce you husband and wife. Drew, you may now kiss your bride."

Zach watched his best friend bend his new wife over his arm and give her the hottest kiss he'd ever seen in a wedding. After nearly a minute, Zach tapped Drew on the shoulder and the couple stood.

The minister quietly thanked Zach for interrupting the kiss and said, "Friends, may I be the first to introduce you to Mr. and Mrs. Drew Kipling." Drew swept Lily up in his arms and charged down the aisle. Zach shook his head at the minister, who shrugged. The rest of the people assembled laughed at Drew stealing away with his bride.

Zach followed the couple with Lily's maid of honor on his arm. She was a pretty girl. He glanced one more time at Emma and was glad to realize his anger toward her had cooled. He didn't need to ruin his best friend's wedding. He would wait until tomorrow or even Monday to have his discussion with Emma. For tonight he would be there for his friend, dance with all the single girls, and pretend he was having fun. Maybe he could convince himself.

He and the maid of honor stood in the reception line. Zach heaved a sigh of relief when Emma did not come through it. He'd been tense the entire time trying to smile and be friendly with people. He wasn't quite sure he pulled it off. Some folks he'd known for years gave him strange looks, so he figured his smile was more of a grimace. The ones he didn't know, from Lily's side, probably thought he always looked like a mean bastard.

Some of the girls he knew from high school tried flirting with him and he told each one to save him a dance, but that's all the niceness he had in him at the moment. As soon as this damn reception line was over, he was heading straight for the bar and a shot of whiskey.

∞∞∞∞

Emma slipped out of the church as quickly as she could. There was no way she was going to go through that reception line. She figured Zach and she would have to have a talk, but it wasn't going to be at her brother's wedding if she could avoid it. She used Tony as an excuse for leaving by the side door. Besides she already knew everyone and could give Lily and her brother a hug later.

Ian followed her, believing she really did need to get Tony away from the crowd. She felt a twinge of guilt about that, but not enough to stand in that line and smile pleasantly at Zach. It might put Tony in a bad light, but he would have to take one for the team, because Emma just couldn't do it. She still had no idea why he'd been so furious, she was the one that had been wronged, not him. The jerk.

She quickly walked down the street to the Grange Hall. Lily and Drew had decided to use the Grange for the reception, rather than the ranch, primarily because it was February. Not only did the house not have a large enough room for a reception, but it could snow at any time and strand everyone at the ranch. Staying in town alleviated the snow risk and the Grange had a nice large area for people to hang out.

When Beau and Alyssa had gotten married it had been warm enough to have the reception outside in big tents, but even then, they'd decided on the Grange because the setup was so much easier. The Grange was close enough to the church that people attending the wedding could park in either lot. She'd parked near it rather than the church, knowing as the day wore on that she would want to be parked closer, when it was over at the end of the day.

Tony was a good kid, but even he could get tired and cranky after such a busy day. She didn't know if Ian had driven or walked, since he had a place in town above his clinic. She didn't really care, but at least it was something to think about, besides Zach.

She asked, "Did you walk over?"

"Yeah, and I think if I'd driven, I would have ended up parking further away than the clinic," Ian said waiving his hand at the street, with every parking spot taken.

Emma forced a laugh. Ian was a good guy and she needed to try to keep up her end of the conversation. He was her client and friend, but sadly there was no spark. No, that particular sensation was fixated on Zach, and Zach alone, she hoped someday that would change.

Dammit, why did he have to still be so good looking? Seeing him standing up there in his tux had made her whole-body flood with heat, until he looked at her with such coldness, then she'd felt frozen clear through.

Well, she was going to sit as far away from the head table and the bar as possible. She didn't want to see him or be anywhere near him. At least he had plenty of responsibilities as the best man. It should keep him occupied, at least at the beginning. Please God, keep him occupied.

"Mama, why are we hurrying so much? How come we didn't stand in that big line to shake hands with everyone like we did at the other weddings?"

Emma slowed her steps. She had been racing along the street, trying to outrun Zach, or her past, or something, her feelings maybe. "Sorry Tony, I was cold, so that's why I was hurrying. And I thought you didn't like standing in the line to shake hands."

Tony frowned. "I don't much like it, but that didn't stop us from doing it at the other weddings."

What could she tell Tony that would make sense to him? She couldn't say she didn't want to face his father. "I just thought you could use a break."

"Thanks, Mama." Tony skipped a couple of steps and then turned back. "Is there a play area set up for us kids this time, so we don't have to sit in the big room or dance with the old people?"

"Yes. There is a kid's room. I think Uncle Drew has some special treats in there for you, too."

"Yay. Let's hurry, then."

Emma laughed and resumed walking faster as Tony tried to race ahead.

Ian took Emma's elbow and she jumped at the touch; she'd nearly forgotten he was with her.

She was acting completely crazy and needed to calm down. She knew Zach well enough to know he wouldn't do anything to disrupt Drew's wedding. At least she thought she knew him that well, but he could have changed in six years.

Ian said, "So what is the hurry? You lit out of that church like Satan himself was on your tail. What's going on, Emma?"

Shit, there was no way she wanted to talk to her date about what she was feeling. First, she didn't know him that well and second, she wasn't interested in him. He was a shield and that was all. But she couldn't exactly tell him that, so she shrugged. "I just thought Tony was getting restless. I guess I was wrong about that. Sometimes mother's intuition is right and sometimes it's dead wrong." She gave a wry chuckle and hoped he bought the act.

Ian raised an eyebrow, he probably didn't buy her BS for one minute, but he didn't press.

She breathed a sigh of relief. "It was a lovely wedding, wasn't it? Drew kissing the hell out of Lily was pretty amusing."

"Who was the guy?"

Had Ian noticed something between her and Zach? She felt her body tense. "What guy?"

"Drew's best man, the guy that finally stopped the marathon kiss."

Emma relaxed, Ian was still on the kiss, thank goodness. "That's Zach McCoy, Drew's best friend and a rodeo cowboy."

"I think I've seen his name mentioned a time or two in the PRCA writeups. He seems to be doing pretty well."

"If you say so. I don't have much time to follow the accounts of the Professional Rodeo Cowboys Association." Liar that she was. She followed every single article for a glimpse of Zach's name, even though he had deserted her and Tony. ProRodeo.com was her top web browser site, but she was not about to admit that to anyone. She didn't want anyone to know how pathetic she really was.

She called out to Tony, who was nearly at the Grange, several yards ahead of them.

Ian scoffed. "How can you not follow it and be from a ranching family? Isn't that like sacrilegious or something?"

"I'm sure my brothers follow it and probably the PBR too. But we breed cattle to eat, not as rodeo livestock."

Ian shrugged. "I have to admit I'm a little partial to the PBR, I love to watch those bullriders."

Emma rolled her eyes even though Ian couldn't see her in the dim light. Most people thought the Professional Bull Riders were the only important part of rodeo. But in her opinion, they left out the best parts. "I'm partial to the ropers and barrel racers myself. My brother and I made a pretty fine team roping pair back in high school. And my mare can still run circles around some of the newer barrel racers. She's getting to old to compete now, but put her in a corral with barrels and she can really move."

Emma was glad that they'd reached their destination, it would give her something to do. They walked into the warm Grange hall, it was very prettily decorated and nearly empty, since she'd not stayed for the reception line and had practically run down the street between the church and the Grange.

The only people present, were the servers and the high schoolers they'd hired to man the children's room, so she could busy herself with Tony to get him settled in the play area. "Ian, why don't you grab us that table in the back?"

She pointed to a table far away from the front of the room, so she wouldn't have to see Zach. She was not the least bit sad to have raced down to the reception, so that they had their pick of tables.

Ian's surprised expression didn't bode well for him not asking questions she didn't want to answer, so she whisked Tony away to the kid's playroom. Maybe by the time she got back, he would have forgotten. She could hope so anyway.

Chapter 3

The first thing Zach did when they got to the Grange was head to the bar. He asked for two shots. After paying, he slammed one and then carried the other away to sip. That's all he was having, he wasn't allowing himself any more than that, he had best man duties to perform, which included a toast to his best friend and his girl.

The more important duty, as far as drinking was concerned, was driving said best friend and his new wife to the cabin they planned to spend the next two nights in.

Drew had told him all about how he'd found Lily and they had spent the first few days in the cabin. He and Drew had gone to set it up for the wedding night with plenty of flowers and candles and decadent food. They'd done a good job, too, as far as he was concerned. The love nest was complete.

Drew had brought both his and Lily's horses

out, so they could ride if they wanted to. Zach didn't figure they'd do much horseback riding. Another kind of riding, yep, there would be a lot of that going on in the cabin far away from the house.

Zach weaved his way through the people back up to the front table where he and Lily's friend, Kathy, would sit next to the bride and groom and do whatever was needed. When the dancing started, Zach and Kathy would dance together when it was time to signal to the others that they could start dancing.

Kathy was a pretty girl, but Zach wasn't interested in starting anything with a woman. He was focused on his career and didn't need the distraction. Besides that, he already had a five-year-old distraction that he was going to have to get to the bottom of. But not tonight, that was going to happen after he got his best friend on an airplane and heading somewhere else. So, to keep himself occupied, he was going to dance with all the girls, not single out just one, that way no one could get the wrong idea. He didn't want to watch Emma with that other guy and the only way to prevent that was to dance.

After a delicious dinner of Kipling beef and enough side dishes to feed a lot more than the couple of hundred ranch hands assembled, the party really got started. There were toasts and stories galore as the new bride and groom were feted.

Zach managed to give a toast in their honor that included his best friend for sixteen years and his lovely bride, whom he knew more through her father's horses than anything else. Although he'd certainly heard of the horse rescue Lily worked at. He got one little dig in about not being called to help protect Lily when they'd been in New York, and how Drew must have forgotten the best friend rule, of being the wing-man in all situations.

Someone had gotten a copy of the clip where they had taken down Bubba Pamper, aka Baby Pooper, when he'd tried to skew the results of the beauty pageant, by preventing Lily and the other Rocky Mountain contestants from competing, using many nefarious means. The whole room rang with laughter as Cade had roped the man, Summer swept his feet out from under him, and Drew hogtied him. The clip had gone viral and the three of them had become overnight sensations. Sales of ropes had gone up and the you-tube video clips on how to tie a rope had gone way up in views.

As the party continued there was a slide show with pictures of both families, and also their time in New York. Zach was in a lot of the Kipling pictures hanging out with Drew. Zach noticed a few where his concentration was not focused on what he and Drew were doing as much as on Emma, which pissed him off.

He was glad when the dancing started so he

didn't have to see his own stupid moonstruck face projected on the wall for everyone to see. He just hoped no one else had seen his cow-eyed expression or at least didn't know what it was all about, since Emma herself had not been in many of the pictures. But he remembered exactly where she had been standing and what she'd even had on. Yeah, he'd had it bad, back then. But those days were past. Firmly passed.

Even if he could describe in explicit detail what she had on tonight, dammit.

She'd been a beauty in high school, but the adult version of Emma was way beyond beautiful, her shape was rounder, softer, probably from having Tony. Not fat, but mouthwateringly perfect. She'd lost the younger facial features, also, and was stunning. The dress she had on clung in all the right places and flared at the knee. God he was such a damn fool.

He sighed a breath of relief when he got the signal to start the rest of the crowd dancing and moved the pretty maid of honor out onto the dance floor. For a moment he couldn't remember her name, but before he made an ass out of himself it came to him, Kathy, the girl's name was Kathy.

He whispered, "I promise not to step on your toes, Kathy."

She laughed. It was a pleasant laugh, but it did absolutely nothing for him. She looked up from under her lashes. "I'm going to hold you to that, because I already took off those torture devices masquerading as shoes. I might be Lily's maid of honor, but I am no beauty pageant contestant. Just a good old country girl and rodeo fan."

He grinned down at her. "Are you now, what's your favorite event?"

"You're going to think I'm weird since it's not the bulls. I prefer bulldogging."

"I don't think it's weird at all, it gets kind of old that so much attention goes to the bulls. Not that I don't like that part also. But the bulldogging is a completely different type of competition."

"You do a fine job at it."

"Thank you, I'm trying to do a fine job in both my events."

"Yeah, all-around cowboy would look good on you."

Was she coming on to him? Possibly, but he didn't want to engage in anything. He had business to take care of while he was here. Fortunately, the music was coming to an end. He saw one of the girls he'd doubled with a few times back when Drew was with Monica. She'd be safe. "Thanks for the vote of confidence. I'd like to have another dance, later in the evening if you are interested. I've got some friends to mingle with. I haven't been back here in six years, got lots to catch up on."

She sighed and looked around. "All right, I'll see what my dance card looks like later. But remember, Kathy from Montana will be watching your every move, so I want to see some mighty fine bulldogging, cowboy."

He chuckled. "Yes ma'am, I'll keep that in mind."

Kathy went off to dance with someone else she knew, and he caught Julie's eye, with a nod toward the dance floor. She smiled, then walked out to join him.

"Hi Zach, it's good to have you back in town." Tears filled her eyes. "I am so glad that Drew has found someone again."

Dammit, Julie was one of the criers, he'd forgotten that. Drew had complained many times about all the girls from Monica's clique tearing up every time they saw him. The woman had been dead for, was it seven years now, no eight, and those girls were acting like it was yesterday. He wanted to roll his eyes and tell her to move on already, but instead he pulled his handkerchief out and handed it to Julie. "Yeah, I'm happy to see he's found someone to love again. So, what are you doing these days?"

The tears dried up quickly when she started talking about her job as a tour guide in the summer and an outfitter in the winter. She also did a lot of the scheduling for the company. He kept her talking by asking strategic questions. When the song was over, he was a little more strategic on finding the next dance partner. In other words, not one of Monica's friends, in fact it was some girl from Montana, he'd never set eyes on.

He introduced himself and asked if she'd like to dance. She quickly agreed, but it wasn't thirty seconds into the dance before she teared up too and started babbling about Lily's best friend Olivia. She said she was pleased that through Olivia's death Lily had managed to find her true soul mate.

He didn't have another handkerchief to give this girl, he spied an unused napkin on a nearby table and snagged it to give her. She smiled up at him through watery eyes. Fuck. Was every female he danced with going to start bawling? Maybe he should go to the bar and grab a stack of napkins to hand out. He might just head back to Kathy sooner than he'd planned if this was going to be the case.

He started scoping out the next partner before the song ended, he needed to get away from the waterworks.

There was always Sharon. She didn't have a compassionate bone in her body. He wasn't completely sure he was ready for the octopus however; the woman had more hands than anyone and she wasn't the least bit shy about groping a man, even in public. He looked around the room and didn't see anyone else he could trust not to burst into tears. Sharon it was.

Sharon saw him glance at her and was halfway across the room before the song was over. Before he could escort the girl from Montana back to her table, Sharon had taken hold of his arm.

"My turn."

What a shitty damn night this was turning out to be. In fact, it rated right up next to the night Drew had called to tell him Emma was pregnant. But he gave Sharon the best smile he could muster, and the song started, of course with his luck tonight, it was a slow ballad.

Sharon got a gleam in her eye and snuggled in close. Dammit all to hell, it was either waterworks or the boa constrictor. Wasn't there one single woman in the room that was sane?

His brain flashed him a picture of Emma, fuck no, not her. He was clearly doomed.

∞∞∞∞

Emma left the ladies' room and skid to an abrupt halt when she saw Zach in all his sexy glory leaning against the wall. He'd removed the tie and undone the first few buttons on his shirt which caused her gaze to go immediately to his chest. Wrenching her eyes away from the sight, she flipped her hair and said in her coldest voice, "Sharon's not in the bathroom."

His eyes narrowed, and he sneered at her. "I'm not waiting for Sharon. I'm waiting for you. We need to talk."

She replied as flippantly as she could manage. "If we must. But not here, not now."

"No. Monday, after Drew and Lily leave on their honeymoon and all the Montana people have cleared out."

"Fine, where?"

"I was thinking about the end of Serendipity."

Remote, far enough away that no one would hear them. "That works. I can be there by nine-thirty."

He nodded once and walked away. Emma went back into the ladies' room to get her hands to stop shaking. She absolutely hated that he had the power to make her shake like that. The question was, what caused the shaking, anger or lust, because as pissed as she was at him, he was still the only man that made her weak in the knees.

And after six years he was even better looking than he had been, and a lot more dangerous. He'd filled out, his shoulders were broader than they had been, his arms so big under the coat that he was straining the seams. His face had gotten leaner and more angled, the trim beard was sexy as hell. The suntan he sported made his blue eyes gleam. She'd deliberately tried not to look at his ass and the tux jacket had assisted her with that, but he had powerful legs that the tux pants couldn't hide.

She really didn't want to return to the party to make excuses to Ian why she didn't want to dance. She loved to dance, but she wasn't the least bit interested to join in on the floor with Zach dancing with every single girl there, especially Sharon.

This was an evening of pure torture. She was beginning to wish she'd never invited Ian. He was trying to be amusing and entertaining. He was considerate, and brought her drinks and cake. He'd asked her to dance several times and he'd even gone with her to check on Tony, who was having an excellent time with the other kids.

But he wasn't Zach. And it didn't matter one bit that Zach had abandoned her and Tony. She wanted to be the one in his arms out there on the dance floor. Dammit.

Chapter 4

Emma wiped her sweaty palms on her jeans as she waited for Zach. They were meeting in the National Forest far away from everyone, at the end of a dirt road. She'd gotten Tony off to school and had made some lame excuse about needing to go to Granby to work with a client.

She didn't want to meet with Zach, especially after him acting like a horn dog at Drew's wedding, dancing with every single female in attendance, especially Sharon. Sharon had always wanted to sink her claws into him. He'd continually blown her off before. Well, he could have the slut. He'd be just one more notch on her bedpost.

Ian had finally coaxed her out onto the floor and who had Zach been with? Yep, Sharon, and boy had she sent Emma a smug smile. She'd wanted to slap that expression right off of her face, but she didn't think Drew would appreciate a cat fight in the middle of his wedding reception, and Lily would have... she wasn't quite sure if Lily would have been mortified or would have joined Emma.

The thought of Lily in her wedding dress helping her slap the hell out of Sharon put a smile on her face, just as Zach drove up. The smile slowly faded as he turned off his big, fancy, top of the line, extended cab truck and stepped out of it.

Why, oh why, did he have to look so good? Zach was just a handful of inches taller than herself, but those inches were just damn sexy. He was built with strong arms and broad shoulders, tapering to his waist and then... Whew, the man filled out his jeans in all the right places.

She looked up to see him watching her. The tight t-shirt emphasized his muscles and was a baby blue that made his blue eyes stand out even more than normal. Her fingers itched to feel his beard, was it soft or stiff? Well her fingers were not going to find out, bad fingers that they were, she was keeping them far away from Zach McCoy.

Emma was glad she'd worn sunglasses and her hat, maybe he hadn't noticed her slow perusal. He'd looked mighty fine in his tux, but in the jeans and blue t-shirt, well, she was afraid she might drool, except her mouth had dried up enough to resemble an alpine desert. Had fear or anger caused it, that was the question?

She went on the defensive. "Well better late than never, I suppose."

He pulled out his phone. "I'm right on time."

"Today."

He frowned. "What's that supposed to mean?"

"Oh, nothing at all Mister Rodeo. Wouldn't want a little thing like a child to stop you from competing, even if you did tell me the only reason you were leaving was to let me grow up. Well, mission accomplished."

"What in the hell are you talking about? I never said any such thing to you."

Fucking liar. "Oh gee, I must have made that up. So, are you telling me it's not true? That you never planned to come back? That rodeo was in your bones, because that would at least be an excuse that I could handle. Rodeo is a great career and I have no problem whatsoever with you wanting to compete. But dammit, Zach, I'd have gladly climbed in that fucking truck with you and lived on the circuit. But you didn't give me that choice, instead you abandoned me, and Tony."

Zach pulled his hat off his head and slapped it on his leg. "What in the hell are you talking about Emma? I didn't abandon you. I didn't even know Tony was mine until he walked down that aisle looking exactly like I did at that age, wildly curly hair and all."

She folded her arms across her chest and glared. "Drew said he called you."

Zach put his hat back on his head and said in a rough voice, "He did. He told me some drifter had gotten you pregnant and left you high and dry."

"Well, wasn't that a convenient excuse for you? Besides, I never said that, I just didn't tell them it was you. I told them the father was gone, which you were."

"We never had sex, Emma. How can Tony be mine?"

She marched over and poked him in the chest. "We sure as hell *did* have sex."

He clamped his jaw shut and gritted out. "No, we did not."

She would have poked him again, but the first time had hurt her finger, so she turned her back on him and stalked away. Emma turned around and said in her nastiest tone of voice. "I never figured you for a liar, Zach. A deadbeat father, yes. A man that made promises he didn't keep, sure. But a liar, nope, I never would have guessed."

"Emma, wait. At the risk of sounding like an ass, I truly don't remember ever having sex with you."

Zach had either become a hell of a good actor or he honestly believed what he was saying. She could not for the life of her figure out how he couldn't know.

He continued, sounding completely confused. "I wanted to, and you're right, that *is* why I left. I was afraid I couldn't keep my hands off of you until you graduated and had time to decide what you wanted."

He'd told her that exact same thing, the night Tony was conceived.

He looked at her with a pleading expression. "Tell me. When did we have sex? How was Tony created?"

"The night before you left, at your going away party."

"On the plateau? But I know I went to bed alone. I was pretty wasted, but not that bad. I know I went to my tent alone."

"Yes, you did, but when everyone was busy or in their own tents, I came into yours. You were happy to see me. You told me all about your reasons for leaving and insisted we couldn't be together."

He shook his head then took off his hat to run his fingers through his hair. He sounded so sincere when he said. "I don't remember. Are you sure I was awake?"

"You were talking to me. Of course, you were awake." What a stupid question, did he think she was an idiot?

Zach frowned but motioned for her to continue with the story. "I told you I wanted one night with you before you left. I was so damn afraid you would meet some woman on the circuit, a buckle bunny or another competitor and never look back."

"Emma, no, I loved you."

She winced at the past tense. "Well, I wasn't secure enough to believe those words then. So, we had sex. I brought condoms with me that I stole from the wedding-after party for Kristine and Daniel."

His face showed nothing but confusion. "I honestly don't remember a thing." If she hadn't been there that night, she would have believed him.

She honestly thought she would rather have him lie to her, than really not remember. Was she that unforgettable? Dammit, now it was her that had been lacking, not Zach. Although if she was honest she'd wondered if he'd felt she was lacking and that's why he hadn't come back. She did not like the confirmation. She had to get away from him before she broke down, she could feel her self-control starting to slip.

"Well fine, if that's the way you want to play this, I've got nothing else to say. Go spend the rest of your time here with Sharon." She stormed over to her car. She wasn't going to look at his lying face one more minute.

Zach called out as she turned the car on, "I'm not interested in Sharon."

Emma rolled her window all the way down and glared at him. "Well, you have a funny way of showing that." Then she slammed on the gas, dirt and rocks flew into the air as she sped away.

She wasn't going to cry dammit. The most magical night of her life and he didn't remember? What an ass. Was he lying to her? She didn't get it. All those things he'd said to her. Were they all just lies?

There was no way she would give him the satisfaction of seeing her cry. Emma drove to the end of Serendipity and took another back road that wound further into the national forest. She found a quiet spot where no one but hunters or maybe fishermen would be and drove her car under a tree for some shade and privacy, then she let her feelings pour out.

Emma wouldn't let Zach ever find out, but he'd gutted her. Even though it had been six years since he'd walked away, she'd still held out a tiny bit of hope that... what? He'd been confused? He'd been building them a nest egg? Stupid, she was just damn stupid to have held onto the dream, the idea of her and Zach together.

Didn't remember? What a crock of crap! What did he take her for? A moron? He'd talked to her; his body had been ready for hers. Yes, he'd been more passive than she'd expected but she'd been happy to take the lead. Thrilled even that he'd let her have the reins.

Couldn't remember? It had been her name on his lips when he'd come. Asshole. She never wanted to see his lying face again. And if he all of a sudden decided he wanted visitation rights, well then, he'd have to take her to court. The jerk.

Her anger shuddered to a halt. What if he did want to see Tony? She couldn't bear to have Tony go with his father on the road. No, she wouldn't allow it. But she knew in her heart that if Zach wanted visitation it wouldn't matter whether she wanted it or not, the courts would give it to him.

Dammit, she'd been the one to carry Tony in her body. She'd been the one to soothe him when he was teething or had a cold. Not Zach, all he'd been was the sperm donor, who couldn't remember. What a mess.

∞∞∞

Zach stood perfectly still as Emma raced away from him. He couldn't move. He should have gone after her, but he couldn't wrap his head around what she'd told him.

When he'd first driven up and she'd looked at him with that sweet smile on her face he'd been overcome with joy at seeing her. Then he'd stepped out of his truck and the smile had faded, but he'd felt her gaze roam over his body. It had been as hot as the noon-day sun in Arizona. She'd wanted him, and it had sparked an answering desire in himself.

He'd wished they could have stopped time right at that moment. But no, it had marched right along, and she'd ripped him a new one. Only it had been centered around his heart. He could not figure out what had happened.

He thought back to that night six long years ago. He'd been torn up about leaving her, but determined it was for the best. His friends had thrown him a going away party that had included plenty of alcohol. Zach didn't know which of Drew's brothers had bought the booze, but Drew had taken keys away from every single one of them before he let them have one drop. No one was drinking and driving on his watch. Drew had lost his long-time girlfriend to a drunk driver, which is why he'd gone to the police academy right out of high school and had been getting his degree in criminology, rather than the business degree he'd planned on getting.

Zach had had plenty to drink. He'd tried to act jovial as his friends ribbed him about running off to join the circus. But in truth his heart had been breaking. He didn't want to leave Emma or what had become his hometown.

He did love the rodeo and if he had to leave Emma it was the only thing he would consider doing. Zach was pretty good at it back then, and had honed it over the years into a damn fine career. A lonely one, but still, he wasn't interested in settling down, not with anyone besides Emma.

Turning his thoughts back to that night. Zach remembered going into his tent, dragging off his jeans and passing out on top of his sleeping bag. He'd not even managed to crawl inside it. He'd been exhausted from sorrow, booze, and pretending to be his normally happy self.

The next morning he'd woken with a headache from the booze, still on top of his sleeping bag. He'd been cold and had pulled on his clothes and a warm jacket. Then he'd sat in his tent for a few minutes and marveled at the erotic dreams he'd had of Emma.

Fuck, those hadn't been dreams. It had been real, but he still didn't remember being awake, they had felt like dreams. But he'd obviously talked to her and told her the truth he'd been hiding from everyone. He'd been fairly certain Drew had figured it out, but he'd known him the longest and best.

It hit him like a bolt of lightning. Drew had always laughed about Zach talking in his sleep when he was the most exhausted. Had he talked to Emma in his sleep? Yeah, that was probably what had happened. And since he'd been in the middle of an erotic dream his body would have been happy to comply.

Dammit, he'd made love to the woman of his dreams for the very first-time sound-fucking-asleep. Well, hell.

And what had she said about condoms? He'd been too flabbergasted by what she'd related to be paying attention. Something about stealing them. Oh, fuck no, she'd stolen them from Kristine and Daniel's party. She had stolen the ones they had poked holes in and had given to Daniel as a stupid gag gift. Daniel had known they were worthless, but Emma wouldn't have.

Zach threw his hat in the dirt and kicked a tire on his truck. What a comedy of fucking errors.

So now what? Did he try to talk to Emma again and explain? One thing was for certain, he might just punch his best friend in the nose for being a damn idiot and telling him a bunch of bullshit. *Drifter, my ass.*

Chapter 5

D rew had been back from his honeymoon for two days and Zach figured it was time to have a chat with his best friend. He'd gotten the letter from his mom a few days ago. He texted Drew to see if he could take a ride with him up to the plateau. Drew was enthusiastic about that idea, and said Lily was taking the day to settle in some of the things her parents had brought down from Montana, and making his room, into their room. They were going to stay in Colorado at least for a few more months, after that, their plans were still up in the air.

Zach and Drew rode across the ranch in companionable silence. Zach didn't want to say anything until they were far away from any listening ears. They rode up onto the plateau and sat on a log overlooking the ranch. They each opened a bottle of beer and clinked the necks together like they'd done for years, even though for most of those years it had been root beer.

Zach said, "I've got a bone to pick with you, and I imagine you'll have one to pick with me when I'm finished."

Drew turned his head slowly with one eyebrow raised. "Okay, pick away."

Zach reached in his shirt pocket, pulled out the picture his mom had sent, and handed it to his best friend.

"A picture of Tony, cute."

"Look closer, officer."

"Officer?"

Zach shrugged.

"All right, using my observation skills, I see a little boy about five with curly dark blond hair. It's cut a little different than it was for the wedding, more Justin Timberlake-ish."

Justin Timberlake? Seriously? That wasn't a teenage girl in the picture. Zach muttered, "Tarzan."

Drew brought the picture closer. "I've never seen that outfit before either. It looks like Tarzan from the Disney movie, when we were little. Blue eyes, what the fuck? Tony has brown eyes. These are about the same color as yours..."

"Yep, you got it, Einstein, that's me."

"Then Tony is..."

"Yep, my son. You fucking told me some

stranger knocked up Emma. You stole five years of my life by being a dumb ass and not asking a question or two." Zach's jaw was clenched so tight he was growling. "Five years of Tony's life I will never get back, and five years of being with Emma. Helping her through the pregnancy, being by her side. I want to knock you into next week."

"But you told me you never slept with Emma. Did you lie to my fucking face then?"

"No goddammit, I didn't know."

"How could you not know? Your dick in my sister." Drew's face had turned red and his fists were clenched.

Zach glared at his buddy. "Don't be crude. It was the last night before I left to join the circuit. You know I'd tied one on pretty heavy. I was not looking forward to leaving the best place I'd ever lived, and you, and Emma. So, I got a little drunk and then crashed in my tent."

"Then what?"

Zach took a deep breath trying to calm down. "I passed out pretty quick and then started having an incredibly erotic dream featuring your sister. Only it wasn't a damn dream. Emma snuck into my tent when everyone else wasn't looking. She started talking to me and thought I was awake."

"Oh, fuck, don't tell me you were talking in

your sleep like you do."

Zach sighed. "That's my take on it. Anyway, I told her I loved her and wanted to make love to her, but didn't feel it was right. The Emma in my dream said it wasn't up to me and proceeded to seduce me into letting go of my control."

Drew chuckled at the audacity of his little sister; she would do as she damn well felt like doing.

"It's not funny, dammit. It was too dark for her to see that I wasn't awake, and she said my body was on board with her plans."

"Well yeah, a man can be fully aroused…"

"I know that, and you know that, but Emma did not. To make matters worse she'd stolen condoms from that after the wedding party for Kristine and Daniel."

"Oh fuck, you've got to be kidding." Drew rubbed both hands over his face. "We poked holes in all those condoms we gave Daniel, it was a gag gift, they knew not to use them."

"Again, you and I knew that, but Emma did not."

Drew groaned. "What a fucked-up mess."

Zach said quietly, "Then when she turned up pregnant, she didn't know what to do. She asked you to tell me about her being pregnant thinking that if I really loved her, I would drop everything and come straight back here. Which I would have."

"God damn it."

"When you told me she was pregnant, I didn't know I'd slept with her. Yes, that dream had been more intense than any previous ones, but I still thought it was a dream. So, I felt betrayed and couldn't face the fact she had gone straight into some other guys arms, the minute I left. My pride told me to stay away from the woman and I listened to it, and your stupid tale, and stayed away."

Zach wanted to punch something or throw something. Six fucking years. He'd been gone, for six years and Emma thought he'd abandoned her. God damn it, wasn't nearly a strong enough expletive for how he felt about the whole thing.

"Fuck man, I had no idea. You're right, I should have asked her why she wanted me to tell you. She'd not really said she'd been with a drifter, one of my brothers said that when she said the father was gone. She didn't deny it, so we all latched onto it. I knew how you felt about her, not in great detail, but I could tell. Some fucking cop I am, the evidence was right before my eyes and I missed it, completely."

"Yeah, you did."

"So, now what?"

"Fuck, I don't know. If the two of us get within three feet of each other, we start fighting.

She's dating that damn doctor and she thinks I was an ass at your wedding dancing with all the other girls, especially..."

"Sharon, yeah I knew that was going to piss her off. Sharon was always trying to catch your attention and rub it in Emma's face."

"Which is exactly *why* I danced with her. You know I've never liked her. Yeah, she's got big tits and back in high school she would put out with anyone. But she's never been my type."

"She still has a revolving door for anything with a dick."

"God dammit, Drew. I want a relationship with my son. I love kids, always have. I don't know if Emma and I can ever get past this. And I have all the fucking rodeo commitments. I can't just walk away. Besides that, I'm good at it, and you know it's a short-term sport."

"How long do you have now?"

"Two to three months, I'd have to be back out on the road by the end of May."

"You've got a lot of hard thinking to do. Look at your contracts maybe talk to your sponsors, tell them the score see if they'll let you out of the contracts?"

"I just don't know. It would take a hell of a lot of doing."

"Tony is worth it."

Yeah and Emma, but Drew knew better than to mention her. "Of course, he is, but this is my career and what if Emma won't let me be a part of his life?"

"Emma's not vindictive."

No, she certainly wasn't, but he'd broken her heart and her trust six years ago. Unintentionally, but it had still happened.

"And do I just turn my back on something I've worked hard to build? And then do what? Go back to being a ranch hand here on the Rockin' K?"

"Hell, I don't know. Maybe you could sweet talk Emma into spending part of the season on the road with you. Like the summer, when Tony's not in school. You could come back here in the winter and spring. She could maybe do some road trips in the fall, when you've got something close. Colorado is pretty central to everywhere."

That sounded like heaven to Zach, but he didn't think Emma was going to talk to him at all, let alone go on the road with him. If he got visitation rights, she'd have to let him have Tony part of the summer, but Zach would need help to accomplish that and compete at the same time. "I don't know man; I just don't know."

"Well, you've got a couple of months to work it out. Where are your horses?"

Not at all adverse to changing the subject,

Zach said, "At my sister's, they've got enough land for them."

"If you're going to stay here for a couple of months, we better go get them."

Was he staying? He did want to get to know Tony and he wanted to see if he could at least make amends with Emma. "It's an eighteen-hour drive."

"Yep, and that's too damn far for you to travel to stay on your game. Cade could practice team roping with you, until you find a new partner. We've got plenty of cattle to rope and wrestle. If you want to keep up with other events, Lily's dad breeds rodeo stock, I imagine he's got a cranky bronc or two we could bring down. It's only a ten-hour drive."

Zach laughed. "Guess we've got some trips to plan."

∞∞∞

Emma had been stewing for a week. The same questions going around and around in her head. How could Zach tell her he couldn't remember their night together. Had he been too drunk to remember? But no, she'd heard a man's body didn't perform when he was too drunk to remember. That had not been the case. At all. He had been very much on board, calling out her name, telling her how much he loved her.

And what was that stupid question, was he awake? People didn't talk and make love in their sleep. Well she'd heard of people talking in their sleep or sleep walking, but she didn't think it was quite the same.

Dammit, she needed answers. It wouldn't be hard to get them. He was staying in the bunk house and helping on the ranch. It was getting close to calving season, so an extra pair of hands was always welcome. Thank God, he wasn't coming into the house to eat and was staying out with the ranch hands. Facing him over the dinner table was not something she wanted to do.

That might change now that Drew was back from his honeymoon. She'd seen the two of them ride out this morning. Which wasn't making her feel any better, she supposed they might talk about Tony, if Zach had the balls for it.

She had to admit he had looked a little crazed at the start of the wedding. Was he telling the truth that he hadn't known Tony was his until he walked down the aisle? She was making herself crazy with all these thoughts.

She needed to work or at least do some research. Someone had mentioned that she should be moving her clients' information to the cloud. Emma hadn't even given that a single thought at the time, but the idea was definitely growing on her. It would solve some of the problems she'd run up against.

Like backups that failed to run, or needing to get to a client's information when she wasn't on location. If all the data was on the cloud, she would be able to access it from home. In the winter that would be awesome, there'd been a few times this last winter when she'd had to get out in terrible conditions. Yeah, she really did need to look into it. Might as well get started before Tony got home from school. She needed to see how the transition could be managed. Most of her clients were on the same accounting software. Only Ian and another new client were on something different, so she was working on getting them moved over.

Maybe beginning them on the cloud to start with was a better idea. She'd not gotten too far along on moving either one of them. Ian's books were a disaster, he'd hired someone else to work on them when he'd first moved to town and they had made a mess, and then he'd tried to clean them up, which made it even worse. She was still working through the last little bit on getting them in order.

She'd finally made some progress when Drew walked in the door to her office. It was what had been a small bedroom across from her own room that they'd turned into an office. He shut the door and locked it. Then he walked over grabbing the extra chair she had and brought it around to her side of the desk. Oh no, what was he going to tell her?

She swiveled her chair to face him.

"It's my fault. You need to talk to Zach. I told him it was a drifter. In fact, I ranted and raved about it and all he could do was try to get me to calm down, before I went tearing after... well a figment of my imagination I guess."

Okay, that explained part of it. "But how could he forget?"

"Not forget. He was asleep."

She opened her mouth to protest.

Drew held up a hand to stop her. "Zach talks in his sleep when he's really exhausted. Not just a mumbling word or two, but full-blown conversations. In fact, he talks more in his sleep than he does when he's awake. He spills everything. I used to love it when he'd get that tired. I would pepper him with all kinds of questions, and he just blurts out the truth."

Emma frowned, that explained half of it. "But his body..."

"Responded to you, almost automatically, he's been attracted to you for years. He really was going into the rodeo to give you a couple of years to decide what you wanted out of life."

"I didn't want a couple of years. I wanted Zach."

"Yeah, we've all figured that out, now. Oh, and the condoms. They were a gag gift for Daniel, we poked holes in all of them. Daniel knew that."

"I didn't." Emma huffed and tipped her chair backward looking up at the ceiling. Why? Why had she been so stupid? Stupid seventeen-year-old girl, making love to a man who was asleep, using faulty condoms. She didn't know whether to laugh or cry at the absurdity of it all. She sure as hell didn't want to face Zach.

"So now what?"

Drew shrugged. "That will be up to you and Zach. He wants to get to know Tony. He's planning to stay here until the end of May when he's got commitments to the rodeo and his sponsors. He's damn good at rodeoing and he's made a good career of it."

Three months, he was going to be living on the ranch for three months. Could she handle that? Did she want to handle that? Maybe she should get an apartment in town. No that was a chicken-shit way to proceed, plus she supposed it would be good for Tony to get to know his father.

"Fine, I'll talk to him."

"Now?"

Shit. Now? She needed time to think about

everything. But then if she did that, she would blow it all up in her mind. Maybe it was better to get it over with. She sighed. "I suppose."

Drew whipped out his phone and his fingers flew over the text. She heard an answering text. "He's on his way. Want me to stay until he gets here?"

"No, go away."

Chapter 6

As soon as Drew left the room, she ran to the bathroom that was between her office and Drew's room. She wasn't about to talk to Zach without at least checking to make sure she didn't have food in her teeth.

She checked her teeth, splashed water on her face. Fluffed her hair and checked her clothes to make sure they weren't too ratty. That's about all she had time for, if she wanted to be back at her desk by the time Zach got there.

She sure as hell didn't want him to think she was primping for him. She raced back in, prepared to rush behind her desk and then changed her mind. She stopped in the middle of the room, hands on her hips and waited with what she hoped looked like an aggressive attitude.

She wasn't going to cower behind her desk. Having the desk as a barrier between them might have been good, but she wasn't going to have him looming over her. So, face to face it was going to be.

Zach walked in and she wished she'd gone for the desk, when her knees threatened to give way. He was still the best-looking man she knew, and her brothers were no slouches in the looks department. He'd obviously had a shower and was freshly shaved, primping for her? Or just not wanting to smell like cattle and horses. Regardless, it gave her a tiny boost of confidence.

Did his eyes heat when he saw her? There might have been a flash of something before he schooled his features.

"Emma, your brother..."

"Explained all about your sleep talking and ... other things."

"I really didn't know. I would have been back in an instant. As it is, I feel like I've been cheated of five years with my son... I nearly decked your brother for telling me what he did."

Emma wondered what the pause had been about, was he only interested in Tony or was he going to say something about her too? Maybe it really was just Tony he was interested in. She couldn't totally blame him; Tony was an amazing kid.

Zach shuffled his feet. "So, can we come out of the closet, so to speak, and tell everyone I'm Tony's dad?"

Oh yeah that was going to be a fun conversation. Not. She raised an eyebrow. "Are you ready for the Kipling wrath, Zach?"

"Hell, no. But I'm not going to be a chicken-shit either. He's my son and I plan to be his father."

Emma wanted to ask, 'What about me?' But hell would freeze over before she did. Besides maybe one step at a time was best. She had to learn to trust him again. Plus, after six years, did she even know him at all? Had she ever really known him? She'd thought so. She shook her head. "All right, do you want to come to dinner tonight? Might as well get it all out on the table as quick as possible."

He grimaced. "I guess one big shit storm is better than a dozen smaller ones. What about telling Tony?"

Emma looked at the time. "He'll be here any minute. It might be best to tell him first, so he's not surprised with it at dinner."

Emma heard the door slam and running feet. "Mama, Mama, where are you?"

Emma smiled at her son's enthusiasm and hoped he would be fine, once this next conversation took place. She called out, "In my office, Tony."

Zach looked a little pale. "Mind if I sit?"

She motioned to the chair Drew had used.

"Be my guest."

He pulled the chair out into the room and sat just as Tony skidded into the room. "Look, Mama, I got a smiley-face on my writing today."

Emma went down on her knees to hug her son. It was his first smiley-face on his writing paper, even with all the new thoughts on education, left-handers still had a tough time. "Oh Tony, I am so proud of you. We'll put it on the refrigerator for everyone to see."

"Yay, and can we get a snack while we're down there?"

"Um, how about one of my special cookies I keep up here, in celebration of your smiley-face? Then I want you to meet someone."

"Okay, Mama. I do love your special cookies." He looked toward where Zach was sitting. "That's Uncle D's friend, he was in the wedding. Is that who I'm meeting?"

Well him remembering Zach was Drew's friend would help, since Zach wasn't a complete stranger. "Yes. Let's get you that cookie."

∞∞∞

Zach didn't know what to say or do. He'd had a flashback to his own childhood when he'd had to work so hard to learn to write well enough to make the teachers happy. Obviously, Tony had inherited his left-handedness.

He cleared his throat. "Can I see your smiley-face paper?"

"Sure. I have trouble with writing 'cause I have to use my left hand." The little boy handed Zach his paper.

"I understand. I'm left-handed too."

"You are? I've never met anyone else who is. None of my family is and none of the kids in my class are. I thought it was just me."

"Nope, I'm right there with you. It's not easy being a lefty, but you're doing a good job by what I see on this paper."

Tony took a huge bite of the double chunk cookie Emma had given him. "Thanks." Cookie crumbs sprayed Zach and he grinned at Tony.

Emma said, "Tony, no talking with your mouth full."

Tony finished chewing and swallowed. "Sorry, Mama. But I didn't want to be rude to Uncle D's friend by not answering him."

Emma sighed, "He would have waited until you swallowed, and his name is Zach."

Tony who'd taken another bite chewed and swallowed before he said, "Zach. I've not met any-one with a Z before. My name is Tony, with a T."

Then he stuck out his chocolate-covered hand.

Zach wanted to laugh out loud. The kid was adorable and really smart, knowing his name started with a Z. He was only in kindergarten. He shook the tiny hand and had to grin when his hand was covered in chocolate.

Emma rolled her eyes when Zach licked the chocolate off his fingers. He was certain she was fighting the desire to tell Tony that you shouldn't shake hands that were covered in chocolate, but knew Tony would say he was just being polite.

Zach looked her in the eyes. "Manners are tricky."

She sighed, but he saw a small smile flit over her lips.

After Tony was finished with his treat, she sent him to the bathroom to wash up.

When Tony came out of the bathroom he said, "So, can I go play now? I met Mr. Z."

"Not yet Tony, there's more you need to know about Zach."

She went back down on her knees and had Tony stand in front of her. "You know you've asked me who your father is?"

Tony nodded.

"Tony, Zach is your father."

Tony gave him a side glance. "Are you sure,

Mama?"

"Yes Tony, very sure."

Tony frowned and turned to Zach. "So, where have you been?"

Oh shit, this might be the hardest confrontation of all. Zach swallowed. "I've been in the rodeo."

Tony's frown got darker. "And you didn't have time to come by and see me even once? Or help out my mama so she doesn't have to work so hard?"

Emma spoke before Zach had a chance. "Zach didn't know about you, Tony, or he would have come by and helped out."

Tony folded his little arms across his chest and didn't look the least bit appeased, by his mother's statement. Shit. Zach needed to man up. "Tony, I didn't know, but that's no excuse for me not coming by. I'm going to make it up to you. And your mama. I'm really sorry, can you forgive me? Can I have a do-over?"

Tony looked down at the floor, while Zach held his breath. It was the longest eight seconds of his life.

Tony finally looked up, uncrossed his arms, smiled, and nodded. "Yes, I forgive you, and you can have a do-over. But you have to promise to teach me some rodeo tricks." Then he looked up at his mother. "And help mama."

Zach let out the breath he'd been holding. "I promise to do both of those things, Tony. I'm going to drive over to my sister's place in a few days to bring my horses back here, so I can keep practicing while I stay here to be with you... and your mama."

"All right." He looked at his mother. "Mama, can I go play now?"

"Yes. After you give me a hug."

Zach watched as Tony enthusiastically hugged his mother and then raced out the door. Zach yearned with his whole being for a hug like that from Tony... and Emma. Then Tony was back, he rushed over to Zach and gave him the same hug he'd given his mother, then ran out the door again. Well one out of two wasn't bad. In fact, it had felt damn good.

Emma's eyes were on the door where her son had gone. "Well I guess you're in. With Tony anyway."

Zach grinned. "He's the most important."

"Yeah, until my brothers flatten you like a pancake."

Zach's grin faded as he thought about the evening ahead. "Yeah, you're probably right about that."

Chapter 7

Zach was not looking forward to this evening. He was going to have to explain to the whole Kipling family, at one time, that he was Tony's father. Hellfire and damnation, it was not going to be pretty. He'd been trying to think of a way to broach the subject, since he'd left Emma's office. He'd not come up with a single idea. His brain was mush.

He crossed the yard between the bunkhouse and the main house with trepidation. When he got there everyone had taken their seats, there was only one next to Tony open, with Emma on the other side of the little guy.

Tony's eyes lit up when he walked in and he decided regardless of what happened tonight, that excitement by his son made it all worth it.

Right up until Tony crowed out, "Daddy Z, I saved you a spot by me."

Shit, shit, shit. The room had gone deadly quiet as Zach took the seat next to the happy boy.

Every eye was on his son.

Emma cleared her throat, and every head swiveled in her direction, and she said, "Tony's father is back in town."

Now every single one of them was looking at him. What could he possibly say? Nothing, he couldn't think of a damn thing. He cleared his throat and opened his mouth, but not one word came out.

Drew spoke into the silence. "It's my fault. Emma told me to tell Zach, which I did, but not in the way she'd wanted me to. I told Zach it was some tourist. He honestly didn't know Tony was his, not until the night of my wedding."

Adam's face was purple with rage. "Bullshit, a woman doesn't get pregnant on her own."

Meg said, "Adam, this is not the place to discuss that."

Adam looked at Tony, who was quietly muttering 'bullshit' over and over.

"Fine, but we will be discussing it. Later. In the yard."

Emma spoke again. "No, you will not. It was my fault. I didn't know it at the time, but Zach was asleep. It was my fault."

Adam rolled his eyes. "Yeah, right."

Zach finally had the words. "I didn't know.

But that's no excuse. I loved Emma and I should have come back to support her, regardless of how Tony was conceived. But I was too pis—angry to take the high road and support the woman I professed to love. I plan to rectify that and be a good father to Tony."

He looked at Emma and then each of her brothers. "But if you want to discuss this in the yard later, I'll be there."

Meg cleared her throat. "We would all like to hear a bit more about this subject. But not now. After dinner, we can have a nice chat in the office, once our smiley-face boy goes to bed. Tony, we are all very proud of you getting a smiley-face on your writing paper."

And with that, the discussion was tabled, and everyone fussed over his son, who basked in the praise of his family. His son. That was going to take some getting used to. But Tony was certainly the best part of this whole mess.

The atmosphere during the rest of the dinner was tense. Zach knew the questioning was not going to be fun. He tried to act normal, but it wasn't easy. Zach even managed to get a few bites of food down. It didn't help his churning stomach one bit.

∞∞∞

Hells bells, she knew her family was going to go ape-shit, but Adam had been livid. She figured they'd have some 'splainin to do, as Desi Arnaz playing Ricky Ricardo used to say to Lucy, but she'd not quite anticipated Adam's furor. It wasn't like he'd been the one that was deserted or had been told mis-information, she supposed it was one of his 'oldest sibling' things popping up again.

She hoped Rachel would be able to calm him down while she got Tony tucked into bed. She planned to invite Zach to help her get Tony in bed, so no one punched his lights out. She also wanted to present a united front to her family. She might not have a clue as to what was going to happen over the next few months, but Adam's furor had made her realize Zach was going to be blamed, when in truth it was she that had done it all. She'd practically raped the man.

Zach wasn't treating her that way, but she had to let her family know, even if it did make her look like a slut. She noticed Zach wasn't eating much, probably for the exact same reason she wasn't.

Tony looked at Zach. "Daddy Z, are you gonna read me a bed-time story and help mama tuck me in?"

Emma could have kissed Tony for paving the way. Zach looked at her over Tony's head and she nodded.

"Sure, little man, I would be right proud to read you a story and tuck you in."

Tony looked back at her. "That okay with you, mama?"

"That's a great plan, Tony, and I am perfectly happy with the idea."

Adam muttered under his breath, but she couldn't hear what he said, which was probably all for the better. She looked at her mom who was frowning at Adam. Maybe her mom could calm Adam down before the meeting in the office. She could hope so anyway.

Chapter 8

E mma and Zach left the table immediately, once dinner was finished, and made a bee-line for her and Tony's rooms. Zach wasn't the least bit sad to leave the rest of the group behind. He could breathe easy for a few minutes.

Emma and Tony had rooms that adjoined with a bathroom between them. Tony's room was filled with the things little boys treasured, rocks and pinecones, toys and books, there were posters on the wall of Aquaman and rodeo cowboys. He had a couple of well-loved stuffed animals, and enough toy cars and trucks to fill a huge bin. Maybe one day he and Tony could take them all outside and build a city.

Tony came out of the bathroom after washing his hands, he was a well-behaved boy, Zach was proud of his son.

Tony asked, "Mama, why was everyone so cranky and quiet during dinner?"

Emma gasped.

So much for breathing easier. Tony was also very intelligent and observant. Zach said, "I think everyone was thinking about the fact that I'm your dad. Just like you wondered where I had been, I think they are all wondering about the same thing."

Tony frowned. "But why didn't they just ask like I did?"

"They needed to think about it for a while before they started asking questions, and there's a whole bunch of them, so maybe lots more questions."

Tony frowned, "But why did Uncle A want to go talk in the yard?" Tony looked out the window. "It's kinda dark out there."

Before Zach could think up some way to answer that, Tony asked, "Why did Uncle A say bull poop, not really poop, but I'm not supposed to say the other word. I mean I know that everybody poops, the teacher reads us a story about it when the kids get silly about pooping or farting. So, I know bull's poop, but what did that have to do with you being my dad? Or not knowing that you were my dad?"

Shit, he had no idea what to say to all those questions. He just looked at his son and then out the window and then back to Emma.

Emma interjected, "Uncle Adam likes to take a walk while he talks about things. And I'm not quite sure what he meant by the poop comment. But Nana wanted to wait to talk about those things because she was so proud of your smiley-face paper she wanted to talk about that."

Tony grinned at the smiley-face comment and fortunately let the rest go. Zach heaved a sigh of relief, when Tony said, "Oh, okay. Are we gonna have a bath now? Can Daddy Z help with that, too?"

Emma relaxed and nodded. "Sure, he can." Emma looked at him and there was a mischievous light in her eyes.

He could only guess at what he was getting himself into, but at least they had gotten Tony to think about something besides the dinner conversation. For that he would take on the bathtime challenge.

Forty-five minutes later he was perfectly clear on what her expression had been all about. Tony loved bathtime, and everyone got to share in the experience. Zach was covered head to toe in water and soap bubbles.

Emma smirked when she handed him a towel to try to get some of the water, but it didn't help much.

Tony was now dry and in Aquaman pajamas. Tony was quite taken with Aquaman, which is why he'd begged to let his hair grow long and it was also part of the fascination with bathtime.

Jason Momoa, he was not, but no one had the heart to tell him, in Tony's mind they looked exactly alike. Zach thought he looked closer to the blond Aquaman from the sixties and seventies. He supposed Tony didn't care much which Aquaman he looked like.

The bathtub had been filled with so many toys there was barely room for Tony, but that didn't deter him in the least. Those toys became his minions, to do as Tony commanded, or they would feel his wrath. Which included a lot of splashing.

He read Tony two stories before the little guy started to wind down and get sleepy. In the middle of the third he'd fallen asleep. Zach didn't want the time with Tony to end, it had been an amazing period with the little boy, but he knew he and Emma were expected downstairs. He pulled himself out from under his son, along with the towels that had kept both the bed and Tony dry from Zach's wet clothes, then he leaned down and kissed his child on the forehead, while dragging the blankets up to cover him.

Zach looked over at Emma with awe and gratefulness that she'd allowed him this time. She motioned him to follow her into her room. Emma's room was a reflection of herself. She had a bookcase of novels, he would love to look through, to see what she enjoyed reading. Gorgeous landscapes filled the walls and he wondered if some of them were Rachel's. Her rope, and several cowboy hats hung on hooks on the wall. There was a desk strewn with papers, notebooks, sticky notes and pens.

He tried to keep his gaze away from the bed and focused on the time he'd just spent with Tony. "Thanks, Emma. He's amazing."

Emma nodded. "He is and I'm glad you enjoyed yourself. As far as the inquisition waiting for us downstairs, I want to present a united front to my family. I think the blame for all of this belongs on all three of us. Me for taking advantage of you, and then not being clear and upfront about it. Drew for jumping to conclusions, and you for not, well, not caring enough to come back."

Her voice had hitched on the last, damn, he'd been such a selfish bastard. An immature, self-righteous, selfish bastard. He'd hurt her so deeply; he should have at least come back so she could explain. But no, he'd not given her even a tiny chance. Self-loathing was going to be his best friend for a long, long time.

Zach wanted to go to her and beg her forgiveness, but her stance and attitude told him it would not be welcome. He hoped someday he could make it up to her. No, he vowed, to someday make it up to her. But now was not the time. "Okay, I can live with that. It's mostly what we told them at dinner. And frankly, it's not really any of their business what happened that night in the tent. I don't think we need to go into detail. Let's just tell them that you had defective condoms and I was drunk."

She smiled a sad smile. "That's letting me off too easy."

He shook his head. "No, it's not, you're the one who had to face everyone with an unplanned pregnancy when you were still in high school. You're the one who's had it hard for six years. I'm the one who has had it easy. I'm so damn sorry, Emma. I didn't know, but I still took the chicken-shit way out, and for that, I'm deeply ashamed and totally regretful."

He gestured towards Tony's room. "I've missed out on so much. He's a great kid and I would do anything to turn back time and make a different decision."

"I've thought about that myself, to turn back time to the night you left." She shrugged. "But I wouldn't give up Tony for anything. He's the best thing in my life and even though sometimes it was hard, he's been worth every moment."

"Yeah, I hope you'll let me spend more time with him. Will you, Emma?"

She looked at him for a short moment and then nodded. "Yes. You are his father and although he has a lot of male role models in my family, a father is special. So, yes, I want you to spend time with him."

"Thanks." He grinned. "I'll bring a second set of clothes next time or maybe rain gear and hip waders."

Emma laughed, and the sound shot through him like heat lightning on a summer night. "He does love his bathtime."

∞∞∞∞

Emma had enjoyed watching her son interact with Zach. She'd always wondered what kind of father he would have been. If tonight was any indication, he would have made a wonderful one. She supposed he was still going to make a wonderful one. She just didn't know how it was going to play out.

She didn't want Zach back just because she'd been ignorant enough to get pregnant. Plus, she didn't really know him after such a long time. He'd been great with Tony, yes, but that wasn't the only factor.

As they walked down the hall and then the stairs she said, "Let me lead and don't argue with what I say. I already texted Drew and told him not to contradict us."

Zach frowned but nodded. "I'll go along with what you say, as long as you don't make yourself out to be the bad guy."

They walked into the room together. It was filled with her family.

Grandpa K looked at Zach and guffawed. "Helped Tony take a bath did you, Zach? That boy gets water everywhere but on himself."

"I was thinking rain gear and hip waders might help."

Grandpa K laughed. "Great idea. Not sure how much good it would do. That boy is like a hurricane, throwing water in all directions."

Zach grinned. "He does a mighty fine imitation of Aquaman."

Emma wanted to kiss her grandfather, he'd just gotten everyone to smile thinking of Tony's bath antics, while at the same had pointed out Zach was all in. Zach's happy grin thinking of his son was a bonus.

Before they could bristle back up, she said, "I know you all want an explanation, but first, here are the ground rules. Number one and it's the main one, this is *my* life. It was my decision. You don't get to decide what is, or was, best for me. There were several factors at play and I think we're all going to realize it wasn't any one individual who is to blame. Blame isn't even the right word. I would not go back and change the past for any amount of money or anything else. Tony is the result and I will not be happy if anyone—" she looked around the room at her family, "— anyone acts like he was a mistake."

She paused and watched as several of her family members took that in. "So, the facts are. Zach was leaving, and I didn't want to let him go without one night with him. Rodeoing is a dangerous sport, what if he didn't come back, I wasn't willing to risk it. I waited until he went into his tent after his going away party and when no one was looking, I went in too."

Emma shrugged. "He told me very clearly that he was leaving so he could manage to keep his hands off me. That he loved me and wasn't going to compromise me while I was still in high school. I told him that it wasn't only his choice to make and I wanted one night with him before he left. He didn't kick me out of his tent, so I instigated the encounter."

She folded her arms and looked at Drew and Zach. "What I didn't know, was that the condoms I'd stolen from the wedding party for Daniel and Kristine had been a gag gift, and that the guys poked holes in all of them. Zach was a little wasted, so he didn't fight me off or force me to stop, like he might have, if he'd been sober. But that was just fine with me. It also skewed his memory and he thought he had dreamt the whole thing."

Adam said, "But a man's—"

Emma held up her hand. "He wasn't that drunk; he was still fully functional and very amorous. So, I thought he remembered. Now the next set of circumstances in this tale was you all asking me who the father was. I wasn't going to out Zach until he knew, what I did do was ask Drew to tell Zach I was pregnant."

She put her hands on her hips. "By that time however, you'd all decided it was a drifter. Adam, I think that stupid remark came from you. It hurt my feelings that you would think I was so gullible and slutty, that I would sleep with some tourist, so I didn't correct you. That was my bad, because when Drew called Zach that's what he told him."

She looked at Drew. "I would guess there was a bit of ranting and raving about that, since you were in your first years on the department. A little too black and white."

Drew nodded. "Guilty as charged."

Emma continued. "Zach believed Drew and he felt like I'd betrayed him, plus he thought our encounter was a dream so instead of coming back and finding out the truth, he stayed all butt-hurt."

Emma saw Zach look down at the floor, after she caught a fleeting glimpse of pain in his eyes.

She cleared her throat from the knot that

had formed. "So, in my opinion there is a whole bunch of us that were the contributors to this little drama. Which means Adam, Beau, Chase, and Cade, you will NOT be taking it out on Zach in the yard later. Not one of you stood up for me and fought against the idea that I'd gone to bed with some stranger."

"I started it. You all believed the worst and Drew trumpeted that to Zach, who was hurt by the idea. I'm happy to have my son, and he's thrilled to meet and get to know his father, so that is all there is to it."

She raised her eyebrows and looked at each of her brothers. "Right?"

They shuffled their feet and muttered, then walked out of the room with their spouses.

Her mom, dad, and Grandpa K stayed in the room. Emma figured she and Zach were not quite finished, but at least she'd calmed her brothers down. A little shame did wonders.

Chapter 9

Zach chuckled as he mucked out the stalls in preparation for bringing his horses to the Rockin' K. If he was going to spend his off time here instead of at his sister's place, he would need to bring his horses and all his gear with him.

Tony had been so darn cute this morning, when Zach and Emma, had walked him down the driveway to the bus. Zach didn't feel comfortable going in to have breakfast with the little guy, so he'd waited on the side of the drive until he saw Emma and Tony start down it, then he'd joined them. Tony had been very enthusiastic in his greeting, which made Zach's heart warm.

The boy was outgoing and affectionate. But also, inquisitive, wanting to know why Zach hadn't come to have breakfast with him. He'd had to do some fast thinking to come up with a valid excuse, besides the real reason, which was, he wasn't sure he'd be welcome.

He'd finally decided on a mostly true response, that he'd been making plans to get his horses and rodeo gear to the Rockin' K. Emma had given him an odd look when he'd said that, but he didn't know why exactly.

Emma had been quiet on the walk back up the driveway and then had left to go into town to work. Drew had told him about Emma doing bookkeeping for people and that she was close to being finished with her online classes, so she could take the CPA exam. She'd diligently taken night classes since high school and had been able to add more clients this year, when Tony had gone to school. Zach was so darn proud of her.

He'd been amazed at her standing up to her family last night. Mostly her brothers, she'd always let them lead her around. She was the baby of the family, so it wasn't a surprise that she'd done that. But last night she'd been magnificent and not only because she was defending him. Even if he'd been on the receiving end of her tongue lashing, he'd have enjoyed every minute. Her strength and authority had been a marvel to behold.

She'd not backed down with her parents, either. They'd not quite bought the whole story, seeing through some of the holes in it. But she'd simply told them a bit more of the truth and then said she would appreciate it if they would keep the details to themselves. She'd given each one of the older adults a hug and had whispered in her grandfather's ear which had made the old guy beam with pleasure.

Drew came into the barn just as he was finishing up with the stalls. "I need to go into town real quick. Want to ride along?"

Zach pulled off his work gloves and stuck them in the back pocket of his jeans and grabbed his jacket. "I'm kinda sweaty, but as long as you don't mind, I'd be glad to."

"Not at all, let's go. I was thinking we could have some lunch at the café. Away from the family."

"Fine with me." Zach shrugged.

They climbed in the truck and headed down the drive. Drew didn't wait long to speak. "I noticed you didn't come in for breakfast."

"Yeah, not quite sure where I fit in now. As your friend or a ranch hand I'm good. But as Tony's father, not so much."

"I think that's going to largely depend on you. You can slink around and try to ride under the radar, or you can take your place as his dad. I know Tony would prefer the second. Not sure about Emma, but she sure as hell defended you last night."

Zach chuckled. "She was magnificent."

"She didn't back down, that's for damn sure. I don't think it hurt Adam one bit to be put in his place. Don't get me wrong, he loves Tony and

82

Emma, but you know how he's always been bossy and a know-it-all. Being brought down a peg or two, by his little sister, might be good for him."

"Not sure he won't still punch me in the face when he gets a chance."

"And face Emma's wrath? Nope, I don't think so. Besides, he lives in his own house and he and Rachel don't take many meals with the family, unless they are asked to. Once or twice a week. Beau and Alyssa, too."

"Good to know. I'll give it some thought, joining the family that is." Zach chuckled. "Tony did ask me why I wasn't at breakfast."

"Not a surprise. He's going to want you there."

"I did meet up with them to walk him to the road."

They drove in companionable silence after that.

They walked in the sandwich shop and Jen greeted them both, directing them to the table. When Zach noticed Sharon in a booth watching him with hawk eyes, he almost left Drew to have lunch alone. He didn't want to talk to her. At all.

He'd been so pissed at the wedding that he'd foolishly danced with the woman several times. She'd had her octopus hands all over him and had invited him to come home with her. He'd been damn glad to have driving Drew as an excuse, not that she'd been averse to him coming by after, but he'd managed to put her off.

He sat and pulled the menu up in front of his face, so he didn't have to look at her. He wasn't interested and never had been, he'd just been plain stupid the night of the wedding. Once they'd ordered and he had to surrender his menu, he noticed she was almost finished eating and hoped she had to get back to work. Soon.

Sharon had always done as she damn well felt like doing, so he wasn't a bit surprised when she stopped by their table. "Hi Drew, glad to see you're back from your honeymoon."

She didn't wait for an answer before she leaned over practically shoving her tits in Zach's face. "Zach honey, when are you going to come by and see me?"

Before he could respond, Emma and the guy she'd been with at the wedding walked into the restaurant. The guy had his hand on the small of Emma's back and Zach saw red, or maybe green. But he managed to smile up at Sharon. "Not today, Sharon. You have a nice day."

She narrowed her eyes at him and laughed loudly. "Another time then, Zach honey." Once she'd gotten everyone's attention, she flounced out the door.

Drew rolled his eyes and Zach tried not

to look embarrassed by the woman's antics. He looked around and noticed Emma and the guy had been seated. Emma's body looked tense and her back was turned to him, even though she had to sit in her chair crooked to pull it off.

Drew said, "Damn, that woman is a piece of work."

Zach looked at Drew in confusion.

"She's been trying to get you in her bed since we were teens."

Sharon, he was talking about Sharon. "Yeah, not interested. You would think after ten years; she would take the hint. So, who is that guy with Emma?"

Drew said, "That's our new doctor in town, Ian McDonahue. He's a GP and is planning to open an Urgent Care facility. I hope he does, that forty-minute drive to Granby is a killer when it's something serious."

Zach wanted to groan. A damn doctor, Emma was dating a doctor. He, the rodeo cowboy, didn't stand a chance against a doctor. Fuck.

He didn't want to ask, but he couldn't stop himself. "How long have they been going out?"

"I didn't know they were, until he showed up at my wedding. I thought he was just a client."

Zach didn't know if that was good news or bad.

∞∞∞

Emma was furious. What was that slut Sharon doing shoving her tits in Zach's face? And why had he just smiled up at her with that crooked grin Emma loved so much? Stupid man, he wasn't really going to go down that road now, was he?

She'd been thinking and planning and investigating all day to see what it would take to be able to go with Zach to get his horses and gear. She knew his mom and sister would love to meet Tony; she'd always gotten along with his family in the past.

Tony was only in kindergarten, so him taking a few days off wouldn't hurt anything. The harder part would be to arrange her clients' work, so that her leaving for a few days wouldn't upset them. She would need to get through month end, so if he could wait a week, she could manage it. The only difficult one would be Ian, which is why she'd invited him to go to lunch, so they could talk about her taking a week off.

She tried to sit so she couldn't see Zach and Sharon and her brother, but the way the tables and chairs were arranged it didn't quite work. They ordered drinks and then Ian leaned in. "So, what do I owe the pleasure of your company to?"

She felt her face heat because she realized he

was probably thinking of this as a date lunch, not a business one. "Actually, it's about my bookkeeping for your practice."

His face registered disappointment and he sat back in his chair. "I was hoping for a different reason."

She shrugged. "Sorry. Ian, you're a great guy, but..."

He held up his hand with a rueful expression on his face. "Don't say any more. I don't want to hear it. So, what about my practice?"

"I want to take a week or so off, so I can take Tony to meet his paternal grandmother, aunt and some cousins."

"Oh, but I thought... or had heard... or whatever, that you didn't know Tony's father, or um... at least have any contact with him."

Ian had turned a delightful shade of pink as he'd stammered on about the rumors he'd heard. Emma let him flounder as paybacks for listening to those rumors.

"On the contrary. I always knew who his father was, and I've known his family for years. What I told my family and others was that the father was gone. What I didn't tell anyone, because I didn't know myself, was that the father didn't know about Tony. Let me just say, it was a string of circumstances that no one could have

Shirley Penick

imagined."

"And the father is back now?"

Emma waved her hand towards her brother's table. "He is, as Drew's best friend he didn't have much of a choice."

"Oh, the guy Sharon was tormenting when we walked in."

"The very same. I take it you've met Sharon."

He rolled his eyes. "I'd not been in town more than about five minutes before she made an appointment. It became clear, rapidly, that she was not interested in my professional work as much as she was in my, ahem, other skills."

"Oh, no. She actually propositioned you in your office? As a patient. But that's..."

"Wrong? Tacky? Insane? Pick one. I think they all apply. Needless to say, I showed her the door."

"That won't matter to her much. She's been trying to get Zach for years and years."

"So, you and Zach..."

"Are the parents of a delightful child. We don't know each other anymore, and I don't know if we want to get to know each other again. But he does deserve to be Tony's father and his mom and sister deserve to meet his son. So, can you live

88

without my truly stupendous bookkeeping skills for a week? It would be after month end billing is complete."

"Yes of course. This is important to you and Tony. But until you say otherwise, I am going to continue to hope for more than a client relationship between the two of us."

"I think I can live with that."

Chapter 10

Z ach was only a little surprised when Emma approached him a few minutes before Tony's bus would be arriving. He'd planned to walk down the drive to see his son, even if Emma did not. So, when she appeared at his side as he came out of the bunk house, he was happy to see her, even if she had been with that guy, Ian, for lunch.

She'd changed out of her work clothes and had on worn jeans and a fuzzy sweater that was pink, it made him think of ice cream. He wanted to lick her and see if she tasted like the frozen delight. He doubted it, but knew what she did taste like would be so much better. He turned his attention to anything but licking the woman walking next to him.

They walked side by side down the driveway as he schooled his thoughts. She cleared her throat. "When do you plan to go get your horses and gear?"

"In a week or two, there's no rush. Giving my body and the horses some rest time is good. We rode in Denver in January, so I barely had time to get my horses to my sister's before I needed to head over here." If he'd known what he was going to find at the Rockin' K, he could have had a two-hour drive from the stock show and rodeo and then had a few days to hang with Drew before he got married. As it was, he'd been pushing it to get to Tucson, get his horses settled, and drive back to Granby in the short two weeks he'd had.

"Did you make it into the finals?"

"Yeah in one event, which means I had to stay until the end. I didn't win the finals, but it was good to ride in them."

They were nearing the road where Tony would be dropped off. Emma stopped and faced him. "So, the reason I was asking, is I thought it might be a good time for Tony to meet your mom and sister and her kids."

Whoa, did that mean what he thought it did? She wanted to ride down with him to Tucson? Hours and hours in the truck alone with her, and Tony of course. But still that would be amazing. "As in you and Tony driving down with me and back?"

"Yes. Unless you've already got someone riding with you."

He'd been thinking about seeing if Drew

could ride along to catch up some, but he'd much rather catch up with Emma and Tony. "I think that's a great idea. My mom will love it." As would he, but he wasn't sure if she was ready to hear that.

The bus pulled up and her eyes drilled into him. "You weren't planning to take Sharon with you?"

Sharon, not on a bet. That woman was a menace. "Hell no, what would give you that idea?"

"Well she was all up in your grill at the café and you weren't exactly pushing her away."

"I wasn't exactly encouraging her either. Besides how would you know when you were with the good doctor, Ian?"

Tony ran into her legs about that time and hugged her knees, then turned to do the same to Zach, as the bus let out a belch of smoke and lumbered along to the next stop.

Tony said, "I don't like mama being with Doctor Ian."

Emma rolled her eyes, so Zach asked, "Why not, Tony?"

"Well, he is going to be giving me shots and I don't want to see him all the time. He might decide I need more."

Zach tried to hide his smile from his son. "I don't think that's the way shots work, son. Doctors don't just go around giving shots whenever they please. You only get shots on a schedule or if you need one because your hurt or sick."

"Really, Daddy Z?"

"Really."

"Okay then, mama you can see Doctor Ian, but no kissing."

Emma turned bright red at that statement. "Tony..."

"Cindy says kissing is gross, especially when you don't know the person very well." He glanced between Zach and Emma then continued, "Mom's and dad's kissing is good, except it brings babies."

Now Zach wasn't sure if he wasn't approaching the same color as Emma had turned. Tony didn't seem to notice. "Cindy said babies stink and are all wet and slobbery. And they're noisy and sometimes they puke, too. She said once in a while they smile or laugh and that's kinda fun."

Zach managed to choke out, "So who is this font of wisdom named Cindy?"

Emma laughed, "The girl Tony has to hold hands with when the class goes anywhere outside of their room. I thought you didn't like holding hands with Cindy."

Tony sighed. "I don't, but Grandpa K told me to make the best of it."

"So, you talk about babies and kissing?"

Emma asked with raised brows.

Tony shrugged. "Well we have to talk about something. But sometimes I tell her about bugs and horses. Or tying knots. She likes to talk about how gross babies are, since she has a new little baby brother."

Zach wanted to laugh out loud and a quick glance at Emma showed she was holding in her own mirth. He put his hand on the boy's shoulder. "It's always nice to be a good listener when a girl needs to talk. It's a very important skill to learn."

∞∞∞

Emma didn't quite know what to say or do, Tony had embarrassed the crap out of her. She'd never even hinted at kissing Ian, let alone kissing Zach and having more babies. She'd noticed a bit of color in Zach's cheeks at the mention of other children.

She didn't know if she should say something to her son to discourage his ideas or just let it go. Sometimes letting it go was best, because saying something gave it more emphasis. Or Tony might even dig in even deeper, if she tried to say something wasn't going to happen. Maybe the best course of action was to change the subject.

"Tony, Zach and I were just talking about

the three of us driving down to get his horses. You would be able to meet his mom and sister; they would be another grandma and aunt to you."

Zach said, "And my sister has some kids about your age, so you would have some cousins to play with."

"That would be fun."

"It would be a long drive in the truck. A few days each way, so you would miss a few days of school."

Tony frowned. "I do like school. But meeting a new grandma would be fun. Nana M lets me help her bake cookies. I don't have any other cousins yet; Uncle B and Aunt A are going to give me a cousin in a few months, but it will be a yucky baby first. So, some already grown ones would be better. Okay let's do it. Did you ask the school if I could go, Mama?"

"Not yet, but I will. If we're all decided. I can't go until after I send out all the billing for my clients the first week of the month, so it will give us time to work out all the details."

Tony nodded. "Good. I will have to tell Cindy and my teacher will have to give her someone else to hold hands with while I'm gone."

Emma thought it was adorable that Tony's primary concern was for Cindy. She looked over Tony's head to Zach and he winked at her, he'd apparently come to the same realization.

"I haven't mentioned it to the rest of the family Tony. I wanted to talk to Zach first."

"Okay, Mama, I can tell everyone." And then he took off like a shot down the driveway.

She laughed and shook her head. "Not exactly what I was going for."

Zach chuckled. "Yeah, I guessed that. But Tony's enthusiasm might be the best way. I'm not sure how everyone is going to feel about this idea."

She didn't much give a crap what they thought. This was her life and her son's and she'd kept him away from the other side of his family long enough. They deserved to know her sweet son. "They will simply have to adjust."

"If you say so. My mom will be over the moon. I can't decide whether to call and warn her or to just show up, unannounced."

Emma didn't think the unannounced version was a great idea. "I think some warning would be in order. You didn't take the sight of your son too well, when you first saw him. Your mom might have some of those same feelings. It might be better to talk her through some of them before we arrive."

Zach ran a hand around the back of his neck. "Yeah, you do have a point. But I might wait a few days, so she doesn't nag me to death for two weeks while you get all your clients taken care of."

Emma was amused at his worried tone. "Maybe you could email her the whole story, so she has all the details before you talk to her."

Zach chuckled, "That's not a bad idea. Tell her she can't call until she's read it through at least twice. She knows I talk in my sleep and she should know how a man's body works by now with the proper stimulation."

Emma held up her hand like a stop sign. "Not going to discuss that."

He chuckled again. "I used to sleep walk when I was really little, until I hit first grade."

Emma whipped her head towards him. "Is that where Tony gets it? From you? He's only done it a couple of times; it scared the crap out of me. Him just standing there, not blinking. I've never heard him talk in his sleep, that I can recall, anyway."

"He probably won't then. I did it pretty much from day one. But only when I was super tired."

The things she was learning about her son and Zach. "Interesting."

Chapter 11

By the time they got everything worked out and they were ready to leave, Tony was hopping from foot to foot in excitement, and Emma was ready for a nap, or a drink. It had been the longest two weeks of her life, with Tony asking hundreds of questions while she was working her tail off to get everything ready, so she could be gone for a week.

Her family had been supportive of the idea, at least to her face. Zach hadn't said anything about them saying something to him, so she assumed they'd not been asses to Zach. Drew had whined about missing the road trip, until Lily had lifted one eyebrow at him, then he'd shut up with a quickness.

The best part of the whole time had been Zach pitching in to help with Tony, so she could get her work done. He'd had to field a lot of the questions and she'd been grateful for his help. She wasn't sure she'd have managed it as quickly as she did, if he hadn't essentially taken over the after-school tasks, right up until bedtime. She'd worked late nearly every night, sometimes in her home office and sometimes at the client's.

She was planning to sit back and relax and let Zach do the driving. She thought he'd gone a little crazy buying Tony all kinds of things to keep him occupied on the two-and-a-half-day drive. Zach had bought everything from old fashioned road games, like marking the license plates and finding different items along the route, to hand-held electronic games and movies systems that attached to the headrests.

They were ready to head out and Emma had just now gotten nervous about spending a week or more with Zach. She'd been too busy to think about it, but now that the time was here, she was a basket case, with butterflies swarming in her stomach and her hands were ice cold.

Shit, she should have thought this through a little longer. Maybe made some plans. What were her and Zach going to talk about as they drove hundreds of miles? They couldn't just sit in silence. Maybe she could fall asleep or at least pretend to. She could read on her phone but that would be rude, as would pretending to fall asleep. Damn, she was going to have to think of something to talk about.

Emma realized at that very moment that

she'd never really been alone with Zach, well, except for *that* night. Drew, or one of her other brothers, or a ranch hand, or even her parents had almost always been around. Which only proved to highlight how poorly thought out her desire to be with Zach really had been, back when she was in high school. Six years perspective showed her choices in a very harsh light.

She was committed to this trip however, so it was time to pull up her big girl panties and actually get to know the man who had fathered her child. She hoped he'd really wanted her to ride along and hadn't just gone along with it because she and Tony's enthusiasm had forced him into it. It was too late to change all that now.

Tony charged in the back door. "Let's go, Mama. Daddy Z's truck is all loaded, we're ready to roll."

Her little guy had been dogging Zach's every footstep for the last hour, while Zach loaded all the provisions, they'd gotten together for the road trip. She was fairly certain they could drive for two weeks and not run out of anything. But better safe than sorry. It was still early March, which meant there could be snow anywhere along the drive. "All right Tony, do you need to use the potty before we go?"

"Nope. Me and Daddy Z used the one in the bunk house on the last trip. Daddy Z calls it a *John*,

I don't think my friend John at school would think that's funny, but I do."

She ruffled his hair. "Well I'm ready too, let's head out, pardner."

"Yay!" Tony crowed, and ran out the door, leaving his mother to follow. By the time she'd walked the short distance, Tony had climbed into the truck and was firmly fastened into his booster seat.

Zach grinned at her and she felt her heart flutter. "Our son seems to be a little excited."

She chuckled. "I did notice that. Let's just hope he stays that way longer than the first thirty minutes of the drive and doesn't start with the 'Are we there yet?' question."

"I've tried to alleviate some of that with a map and some colored markers. He's going to mark off certain sections when we get to them. I thought maybe we could chance going through the mountains on the way down, since we haven't had much snow the last week or so and they aren't predicting any for the next few days. It's a little faster route, through Colorado and New Mexico. Then come back through Arizona and Utah which would be easier on the horses and would give Tony new things to look at."

"Sounds fine with me. Since we talked about only driving in three hour stretches your map might keep him busy. Along with all the other toys and crap you bought him."

Zach grinned unashamedly. "I've been saving up the last five years, so he got all his birthday and Christmas presents for the drive."

She laughed. "And it will help keep the very energetic child busy."

"That's the hope. If we get him out of the truck every three hours and let him run around, that might burn off some energy."

Or hype him up, it could go either way, but she didn't want to burst Zach's bubble of hope, so didn't say a word as she climbed up into the truck.

∞∞∞

Zach had tried to prepare for every eventuality for their three-day road trip down to Tucson. He had snacks and games and winter survival gear. He'd suggested to Emma to bring swim suits, so they could use the hotels' indoor pools if they wanted, or stop in Glenwood Springs on the way back, to enjoy the hot springs.

He was ready, and he was pretty certain he had prepared enough to keep Tony occupied. He had possibly gone a little overboard in that respect, but like he'd told Emma he'd not been able to spoil the little guy for five years.

The only thing he'd not given one single

thought to, was sitting side by side with Emma for nine-hundred miles. Basically, alone with his high school crush and the woman he'd planned to marry, for fifty-two hours until they reached his sister's home. And that was just one way.

He didn't know her at all. At least not now. Back then he'd loved her playfulness. He'd loved how she interacted with her family and flirted with him. He'd loved to watch her barrel race or team rope with Cade. He'd loved her carefree spirit. He'd loved her can do attitude.

Zach had no idea if she still had all those traits he'd loved. She was still gorgeous; her chocolate brown eyes snagged his attention whenever their gazes met. Her mouth was made for kissing and her athlete's body made him drool. He wanted to run his fingers through her hair, it was a lighter shade than her brothers and he wondered if it was silky or if the slight curl caused it to be coarse.

None of these observations would help with the drive south. He decided there was plenty he wanted to know about her and Tony's lives so maybe he could pepper her with questions. The alternative was to sit in silence and look like a dumb ass. Yep, questions it would be. If he could think of any. Right now, his mind was blank, in dumb ass mode.

As he got the truck moving, he thought about just coming clean with his apprehensions.

He didn't really want to admit he was feeling like a dumb ass, but maybe it would break the ice or something.

He glanced at Emma. "So, I planned how to keep Tony occupied, but I didn't even think about the two of us. Any suggestions on what to talk about? I'm feeling kind of stupid in that regard."

Emma let out a deep sigh and then laughed. "I'm feeling the same way. I'm so glad it's mutual."

Zach glanced at her with a slight grin. "You, too?"

"Me, too. I realized right before Tony came to get me that you and I have never spent any time alone. We always had people around. Well, except for that one time."

Zach's mind flew to images from that night that he'd thought was a dream. He said in almost a whisper, "Yeah, that one time."

Emma coughed. "Anyway, what about starting with something like twenty questions, but the getting to know you kind. If we can't think of our own questions, I can look it up on my phone. We obviously can skip the things we already know."

He laughed. "That's a good idea. You start."

"Okay..." she tapped a finger to her mouth, lucky finger, "...I know let's start with your sister, how many kids does she have?"

Not what he was expecting, but an easy

place to start. "Natalie has two boys, Wesley is seven and Vernon is six, not quite Irish twins but close. They are both scamps. Once my sister got them both in school, she started nagging poor Alex into trying for a girl. I don't think he fought too hard against the idea, so she's about six and a half months pregnant, and it is indeed a girl. Whether Nat will stop with three is anyone's guess."

"She must love being a mom."

Zach nodded. "She does love it, and mom dotes on them like crazy. My turn, why did you decide to go into accounting?"

Emma shrugged. "I was always good in math, and it was a degree I could get easily with a small child."

Zach frowned. "But you always talked about animal husbandry, like Beau."

"Yes, but uprooting our lives to go to a four year university wasn't something I wanted to do. Without the help of the family it would have been much harder to study and get good grades. You can't take lab classes from home, or over the internet, they have to be done in person, on campus."

Shit, she'd given up her dream for Tony. She reached over and put her hand on his shoulder. "It wasn't a hardship; Tony is the best thing to ever happen to me and I like living in my hometown and near my family."

He glanced at her and saw the sincerity in her eyes and expression and relaxed.

"My turn again."

"Mama?"

"Yes, Tony."

"Do I get a turn?"

"Tony, do you want to ask questions, too?"

"Yes, Mama."

She glanced at Zach and could see he was happy to go along with Tony's request. "Sure, ask away, Tony."

"Daddy Z, what is your middle name?"

Zach grinned at the sweet question. "It's James."

Tony clapped his hands. "That's my middle name too, Daddy Z."

Zach glanced at Emma who was bright red. "It's a most excellent middle name." Then quietly almost under his breath he said to Emma, "Your family is not too bright, are they."

Emma laughed. "Nope, sometimes they are pretty clueless."

"Maybe they would have figured it out if you'd given him my last name."

"I did think about it, but I... well, I just didn't feel right doing it without your knowledge."

He sighed. "Damn. I fu-screwed up so bad. I'm so darn sorry, Emma."

She put her hand on his arm. "I'm sorry, too, for being such a chicken about telling you."

He took one hand off the wheel and squeezed hers for a few precious moments. And prayed that they could somehow get past their mistakes.

Chapter 12

Emma was having a wonderful time with Zach. They'd played twenty questions, well past twenty. They'd talked about the rodeo, what his favorite event was and which one he was the best at. She'd been surprised to hear they were not the same event.

He'd asked about her business and what all she did for her clients. Tony asked about Zach's horses and his family. Zach had asked Tony about school.

Tony had marked off the places on his map as they went through them. And when he got tired of all the talking, had played with his games and watched a kid's movie about Aquaman, on the player strapped to the back of Zach's headrest. He'd also done some coloring in an Aquaman coloring book.

Zach promised to color with Tony on the rodeo cowboy coloring book. She was pretty certain that request had made Zach's whole day.

They'd stopped for lunch in Buena Vista and then had taken Tony over to the Arkansas river, so he could throw some rocks. Zach had tried to teach him to skip them, but Tony wasn't quite adept at that.

When they'd finally gotten back on the road Tony had passed out from all the excitement and activity. So, she and Zach had talked quietly and listened to music. She'd told him the stories about how her siblings had met or at least fell in love with their spouses. Since Tony was still asleep, Zach had to work to keep from laughing out loud at some of the antics.

"You know, Drew told me about some of that, but you tell it much better than he did."

"It's better in person, over the phone a lot of the nuances are missed."

"Maybe, but I just like your version better."

She wasn't sure what to say to that, she'd always felt a little behind her brothers, since she was the baby of the family, so to have Zach say that confused her. She ducked her head. "Thanks."

He took her hand again and squeezed it. Tingles raced up her arm and spread throughout her whole body. When he let go and put his hand back on the wheel, she felt the absence of his touch.

She cleared her throat. "So, do you want to hear the dirt on Drew and Lily?"

He laughed. "Oh absolutely, he didn't say a whole lot about it. Just to get my butt here in time for the wedding. Had to miss a couple of the winter rodeos, but best friends come first. I was kinda ticked he didn't call me to come help in New York."

"He said you were in Las Vegas at some finals."

"I was, but it was to be a spectator, I'm not on the professional bull riding circuit. I've got a good buddy that went with PBR, so I was there in support of him. I'm not one to just do bull riding. I like the timed events better."

"Oh, Drew must have gotten confused. We all know you're ProRodeo."

Zach huffed out a breath. "Well, I did tell him I would be in Vegas and he probably doesn't know the PRCA schedule by heart, so it wouldn't be hard to get the two jumbled."

"Yeah and he took nearly the whole darn family with him, except for me and the elders, so he had plenty of help."

"I saw that clip of Cade roping the guy and then Summer sweeping his feet out from under him and Drew hog-tying him. It was hysterical. It went viral on social media." Zach chuckled.

"It really was. Did Drew tell you about him roping the second guy and threatening to hang him from the catwalk for the rest of the show?"

Zach's eyebrows shot up. "No, he did not. Do tell."

"Well, let me start at the beginning, it will make the end more fun."

"Fine by me. I like hearing you talk."

She didn't know what to think of that statement, so she gathered her thoughts and started the story.

∞∞∞

Zach was having the best day ever, listening to Emma talk about her siblings. He would have been happy to listen to her read the phone book or a dictionary. Her voice soothed him, and she had quite a way of telling a story.

Even if he wasn't enthralled with the woman, he would have enjoyed the heck out of the stories she was telling. She had a keen mind and observed things others might miss. Her sense of irony and humor were finely tuned, and her delivery was excellent. She could easily be a stand-up comedian, at least on the topic of her brothers. He hadn't laughed this much in years.

She wasn't making it easy to stay quiet for Tony's sake. He stuffed down his amusement and asked, "How much longer will Tony sleep?"

She looked at the dash clock. "Maybe another fifteen minutes. He doesn't normally sleep this long, but the truck motion and sound is probably helping him sleep. He was so excited last night. It's hard to say if he slept much."

Zach could relate to that, he'd gone over and over in his head every detail about the trip, trying to remember everything. He wanted it to be a great trip for all three of them. He saw this as his best chance to get to know Emma and see if he could squeeze his way into her life.

"Just as long as he doesn't startle awake, when he gets startled out of a nap, he's a bear. Mom said I was the same way when I was a kid."

"Yeah, I was, too. That's something he gets from both of us, I guess."

She grinned at him and lust shot through his body. He wanted to pull off the side of the road and kiss her breathless. He had to fight that desire and stay on the highway. He internally shook his head; they had a kid together and he'd never even kissed her. At least not that he could remember. What a shitty deal that was.

Her cell phone rang, as she fumbled around for it, Tony woke up. She pulled it out and frowned at the number. "You have the worst possible timing, Ian. You just woke up Tony from a nap."

Dammit what was Doctor Ian calling about?

And what should he do about Tony whining? They were nearly to the exit for the Great Sand Dunes National Park. Maybe a quick stop was in order. It was still early enough in the day they could take a couple of hours and play before they continued on to Taos for the night. Heck, they could even stop in Alamosa if they were having too much fun and didn't want to go all the way to Taos. He'd planned short drives for each day for this very reason, in case Tony needed a little play time.

"Don't lecture me about my son, Dr. McDonahue, you might have letters after your name, but no one knows my child like I do. Now what did you call for?"

Zach wanted to grin at the fact that she was pissed at her boyfriend. Maybe she would break it off with him. Kind of a crappy attitude, but Zach wanted another chance with her.

He said to his son, "Want to see the biggest piles of sand ever?"

Tony stopped whining. "How big?"

"Bigger than ten barns."

He could practically hear the little boy thinking about that. "Are you joshing me, Daddy Z?"

"Nope, want to go see?"

Tony clapped his hands. "Yes, yes, yes."

"Okay, then, hold on." He made a big show of pulling off the highway and Tony laughed in delight.

Emma had put her finger in her ear. She sighed. "We can discuss that when I get back. I told you I will be gone for nine or ten days. You can certainly live without me that long. Goodbye, Ian."

He could still hear the guy talking when she pushed end.

She put the phone back in her purse and then looked around. "Where are we going?"

Tony yelled from the back seat, "To see huge piles of sand, bigger than ten barns."

Zach grinned at his son's enthusiasm and said, "The Great Sand Dunes."

Emma's eyes lit up and she clapped her hands like Tony had done. "Really? I've never seen them and always wanted to. I've lived in Colorado all my life and have never been this far south."

"Well heck, why didn't you tell me you wanted to stop and see stuff? I could have planned better."

"No, we don't really have time to do a lot of sightseeing. Tony has school and I have my clients. Maybe when we come down other times we can stop and see one attraction per trip."

Zach wanted to clap his hands like they'd done. She was planning to come down with him more than just this one time. Take that, doctor fancy-pants Ian.

Chapter 13

Emma was sad to see the last of the sand dunes. They'd had such a fun time. She'd witnessed a side of Zach she'd rarely seen, even when they were kids. He'd been so relaxed and had rough housed with their son. Racing across the dunes then climbing up and sliding down. She was certain both of them had sand everywhere. Bathtime was going to be interesting. She might need a shovel to get all the sand out of the tub when Tony was finished. Zach was on his own.

The thought of Zach in the shower washing away all the sand made her shiver. No. She wasn't going there. That was not the purpose of this trip. He was a rodeo cowboy and would be leaving to start the circuit in May. She had a son in school and a business that kept her busy, and her family, of course.

A little voice niggled. The rodeo was mostly a summer sport. Yes, there were many fall and winter events, but the main ones were in the spring and summer. Tony was only in kindergarten, surely, she could home-school him for a few years. Or he could even attend classes and she could catch up with Zach once the school year was over. If she tried hard enough, she could get her clients all in an online system and come back once a quarter to meet with them face to face. Tax season would be mostly over before the rodeo season started.

No. She needed to stop this foolish speculation. She and Zach were not meant to be. He'd only touched her twice in the hours they'd spent in the car. She'd only touched him twice also. She had to admit those few touches had set her blood boiling. There was still an intense chemistry between them, but that didn't mean it was a lifetime sort of thing.

He probably wouldn't want her and Tony tagging along. Causing him to lose his concentration. No, he wouldn't want them. She needed to get that out of her head.

Zach cut into her thoughts. "I think maybe we should stop for the night in Alamosa. Get us checked into a hotel and try to get most of the sand out of our clothes and bodies. We could either order in a pizza or something, or go out to dinner after we clean up."

Tony said, "Yeah, I am kinda itchy, now."

Zach looked in his rear view. "Me too, pardner. The sand dunes are fun while playing in them, but not so much fun afterwards."

Emma smiled at her son who was scratching his head as sand rained down all over Zach's truck. "We might need to find a vacuum for the back seat."

Zach ran a hand through his own hair and sand scattered. "Front and back seat. But believe me it's seen worse. Mud, blood, horse shit, you name it, it's been in these seats. Nothing a little vacuum and some elbow grease can't deal with."

Emma shook her head. "Good to know you won't be worried about a couple gallons of sand."

Zach laughed. "Not in the least."

"How soon will we get to Amalosa?"

Zach said, "About another twenty minutes and it's Al-a-mo-sa, A-L-A-M-O-S-A."

Tony crowed in delight. "Oh, I see it on my map. And you said the giant sand piles are that big green spot."

"Yes, and they are really called the Great Sand Dunes. Dunes are kind of like a hill made of sand."

"Okay, Daddy Z, I put a heart around the green spot, because it's fun. I think when we're back home, I'll take my map to show and tell. I know Cindy will want to see it."

Zach sent her a quick look and she tried to hide her smile. For all the complaining Tony did about Cindy, she was clearly his best friend. Zach must have been thinking the same thing, he gave her a wry smile and a wink.

Tony was still looking at his map. "So, we missed this part of the street from Moossca to Al-a-mo-sa."

Zach clearly wanted to laugh at his son, but held back. "Yes, we did skip that part, it's called a detour. We detoured into the park to play in the sand."

"I like detours, Daddy Z. Can we do more of them?"

"We'll see about that, Tony. We can't do too many because your grandma and aunt are waiting to meet you."

"And my cousins. I want to meet them too, so maybe only really short detours."

Emma could only smile at her son. He was clearly having a wonderful adventure. Zach was so patient with Tony and had really good ideas about teaching him things.

"I'm gonna watch a movie now."

Zach said, "Put your earbuds in and don't make it too loud."

"Yes sir, Daddy Z."

∞∞∞

Zach couldn't help but grin at Tony's enthusiasm. He was just such a fun little kid. He'd seen other guys with their families, and had on occasion envied them. There were other times that he was glad he didn't have a family tagging along. Sometimes living on the road was tough on he and his animals, and he imagined it would be hard on a family.

He'd not consciously thought about it, but now he reasoned that maybe it's why he'd bought the luxury horse trailer he'd purchased last year. It had sure made this last season run smoother. Not having to pack up all his clothes and live out of a suitcase was just fine with him. The living quarters in the trailer made his life a lot easier, and if truth be told, they were a lot more comfortable than all the different hotel rooms he'd stayed in. And a hell of a lot better than the backseat of his truck.

He figured he'd saved himself a pretty penny not having to rent rooms and eat out all the time. He used campgrounds with hookups whenever he could, so those did have a fee, but being able to whip up a tasty meal in his own kitchen was great. It also allowed him to let the horses out of the trailer when they were in a campground that was horse friendly.

He'd spent some time on the internet finding the best campgrounds near each event and it had paid off, in his mind. His horses were more rested and so was he.

He couldn't help but imagine Emma and Tony in his camper. It was a pleasant thought. They would probably use it on the way back to Colorado and maybe when summer hit, he could take Emma and Tony with him to a few rodeos. Providing she wasn't glued to the doctor.

He already had a hotspot for phone and computer use, so she could maybe keep in contact with her clients. Oh well, all this was most likely a pipe dream. He needed to stay rooted in real life and not let his imagination run away with him.

Emma had been on her phone the last few minutes as his mind had wandered, he had no idea what she was doing.

She finally looked up. "I booked us a hotel toward the edge of town. It has an indoor pool, a small gym with workout equipment, plenty of parking and is near a couple of restaurants. It has room service too, if we want, but that's usually kind of expensive, which is why I wanted one with restaurants nearby."

"Excellent. You can either plug it into the onboard navigation or play Miss GPS yourself."

She smiled. "Your mode of transportation has gone up some, since you left Spirit Lake a half dozen years ago."

"Yeah, my old beater truck did fine the first few years. But when I started winning, I saved it all to put into this baby and then last year I bought a new horse trailer too, the old one was on its last legs."

"Gotta keep up your gear, and that includes transportation."

Zach nodded at her complete understanding. "Exactly. The on-board navigation saved me from a lot of fumbling around trying to find places."

"Yeah. I plan to get it in my next vehicle, right now I just use my phone. My gear is a computer. I've got a good desktop but just recently got myself a brand-spanking-new laptop. Makes a world of difference to use my own equipment rather than the clients'. Eventually I want to get all of their data in the cloud, so I don't have to go to their businesses. When Tony was little it was better to leave the house at night and work in their offices. But now that he's in school, daytime is better, and that's when their offices are busy and not so accessible."

He realized she was much more tied to Spirit Lake than he'd thought, if she had to go to her clients' businesses to get her work done. So, no pipe dreams about her going on the road with him. "Makes sense, plus with Tony gone all day, you probably want to be home with him at night."

"Yep. I've just recently moved one client completely to the cloud. It's a fair amount of work to get it set up, but now that it's done it's so much easier. I can work during the day or after Tony goes to bed. I love the flexibility."

"So, the challenge was worth it."

She chuckled. "I wonder how much quicker a second one will go. I think part of the challenge at getting the first one set up was my own ignorance. When we get back, I'm going to start on the next one and see."

He took her hand and squeezed it. "Well, good luck on that. Now where do I turn?"

Chapter 14

Tony was running back and forth between her room and Zach's, when she came out of the bathroom with her hair still in a towel. She'd had a leisurely shower, had gotten dressed and put on some light makeup, very glad Zach had convinced her to let him have Tony to bathe. Zach had insisted it was silly to get sand all over two bathrooms when both guys could just use his.

She'd still gotten some sand in hers, but nothing like she thought he'd had to deal with. He'd stripped Tony down to his underwear in the parking lot trying to keep some of the sand outside. Tony thought it was great fun to take off most of his clothes outside. Emma had about swallowed her tongue when Zach also stripped most of his clothes off in the parking lot, shaking the sand out of them.

The man was built. His wide shoulders tapered down to a slim waist and hips. His arms and legs so muscular she wanted to lick him like a popsicle. After staring stupidly for several minutes she'd finally mumbled something incoherent and had fled inside the building to check in.

The woman at the front desk had grinned at her. "That's awful nice of your man to try to keep the sand out of the hotel, but being this close to the sand dunes we're used to it."

Emma started to say Zach wasn't her man, but figured the lady wouldn't believe her anyway, so she'd just smiled. She'd given them connecting rooms, explained how to keep the connecting door open 'for the little guy', and with a wink wished her a good night. Emma's face was probably beet red by the time Zach and Tony came in, but thankfully he'd not said anything. And neither did she.

Now they were all clean and Emma started combing out her hair. She'd decided to let it air dry rather than using the hairdryer. She was getting hungry and if she did it properly her hair took a lot of time.

Tony ran back into her room. "Mama, Mama, are you ready? Me and Daddy Z are hungry as bears."

"Two more minutes, Tony. Did you and Zach decide what we are going to eat?"

Tony jumped up and down. "We looked it up on his phone and there's lots of places to eat. Even a place named Emma's. Isn't that funny, Mama? A restaurant with your name. They have tacos and hamburgers and lots of other stuff. Do you want to go there, Mama?"

"That's fine with me, Tony."

Tony went charging back toward Zach's room hollering loud enough to wake the dead. "Yay. Daddy Z, Daddy Z, mama wants to go to Emma's too, but needs two more minutes to comb her hair."

She heard Zach's low rumbling voice.

A few minutes later the guys walked over into her room. Surprisingly, Tony was being quite sedate and speaking in a normal tone of voice, even though she could see he was still vibrating with excitement.

She looked at Zach and raised an eyebrow.

"I just told him he needed to use his inside voice, so they didn't kick us out, because sleeping in the truck is not fun."

"All right, well, let's go feed you hungry bears."

Tony hollered, "Yay" and ran to the door to fling it open.

Zach just watched the boy then turned to her and shrugged. "I tried."

She patted his arm. "Sometimes, that's all

you *can* do."

Emma's turned out to be a nice place with good food, they had pictures of breakfast pastries that looked amazing and some specials that looked so good she wished she lived closer. Tony had kept their waitress hopping but also very entertained. She'd brought him out a tiny scoop of ice cream saying he deserved it for eating all his dinner. Emma groaned internally at the thought of the sugar hyping him up even more.

Zach just winked at her and mouthed, "Pool".

Emma decided that might be a great idea, he did love water and they'd been to Summer's indoor pool a few times, so she knew he could handle it, and they would both be right there with him.

So, she nodded back to Zach, but they didn't tell Tony until they got back to the room. She was glad that Zach had finally realized not to tell Tony about things ahead of time, because it made him too excited.

∞∞∞

Zach was an athlete and worked hard to keep in shape for competition, but he was honestly in awe of Emma and her ability to handle

Tony twenty-four hours a day. The little guy was wearing him out, simply with his enthusiasm. Well and maybe the ten-thousand questions he asked every hour.

Zach had finally learned to keep his big mouth shut and not blurt out what he was thinking to Tony, because once it was said out loud, it was a done deal. Once it was a done deal the enthusiasm and questions shot through the roof.

When Emma had smiled at him for not blurting out the pool idea, he'd thought about what Tony would have done if he had. There would have been a million questions about what the pool looked like and who would be using it and God only knows what else. Then he'd have been ready to leave in that second, not counting for having to pay for the bill or him finishing his ice cream. Then he'd have been hopping in the back seat and running through the hotel.

Yep, this was a good lesson to learn early. He took Emma's lead and noticed she didn't say a word until she handed Tony his swimming suit. Even then the little guy had started in with questions. Emma didn't attempt to answer them, she'd just told Tony to get changed, and had taken her own swim suit into the bathroom.

Zach quickly went over to his room and changed. There was a note in the bathroom saying pool towels were available at the pool. So, all they needed to take was one of the room keys. Their phones could stay in the room, that way Tony wouldn't get them drenched. Zach hoped there wasn't too many other people in the pool, because Tony's enthusiasm would chase them away in a heartbeat.

Speaking of heartbeats, his heart skipped a few when he walked back into Emma's room and saw her in her swim suit. It was pretty modest as they go, not a string bikini but a simple black two piece. Still, she filled it out to perfection, and his mouth went dry.

Maybe they should take some water bottles, preferably cold ones that he could pour over his head, or other places on his body. Fortunately, Emma didn't notice him freeze at the sight of her, since she was putting on Tony's floaties, ignoring the protests that he didn't need them.

Once he could breathe again, he said, "Tony, the more you complain, the less time we'll have at the pool."

Tony looked up at him with eyes as big as saucers and immediately let his mother finish putting on the floaties.

Emma glanced at him the word thanks freezing on her lips as she looked him over, before quickly turning away. He could see a slight flush to her cheeks and was glad to see the attraction wasn't one-sided. He grabbed a couple of water bottles out of the cooler they'd brought in with drinks, glad to have something to do and carry.

Then he made the mistake of letting her and Tony go first and all he could do was stare at Emma's very fine ass as they walked to the pool. This idea to wear Tony out and use up some of his excess energy just might kill Zach. He hoped the pool was cool enough to calm down his raging hormones, but he doubted that would be the case. He wasn't quite sure if the Arctic would be able to accomplish that.

The beauty Emma had become, was astounding. She'd been gorgeous in high school, but the maturity of the woman made her absolutely stunning. Her body had filled out and her hips were rounded, probably from having Tony. Her features had matured and were more defined. He didn't even know how to describe the difference between then and now, but he loved it.

How he'd felt about her then, was magnifying and growing larger with each day, each hour they spent together. He had to find a way to convince her they belonged together, without all the logistics crowding everything else out.

He didn't want to sound like a sap, even to his own ears, but his heart knew they were meant to be together. She was his one and only. He couldn't deny it. He needed to do some hard thinking about how to convince her, that he was *her* one and only.

Zach realized that might have to wait until after the whirlwind that was Tony was asleep. The minute the door was open to the pool area, Tony took off with a shout and jumped right into the water. Zach now understood why Emma had put the floaties on before they left the room.

"I'm going to have to apologize to my mom when we get there, if I was even half as rambunctious as Tony is. Or maybe bring her flowers, or buy her a Corvette."

Emma laughed, and the sound lit up every nerve ending in his body. "I'm sure you should, and maybe your sister, too, since she's older. Now get in that pool with your son and try to keep him from driving away the other people attempting to use it. Thank goodness there's only a few of them. We need to keep him away from the hot tub."

"Yes, ma'am. I'll do my best." Zach didn't dawdle as he went toward the pool to join his son, who was busy splashing in glee.

Chapter 15

Emma put her and Tony's still damp swim-
suits into the small white bag the hotel
provided, and stuck it in their suitcase. She
was torn over the idea of getting another hotel tonight with a swimming pool. It had worn Tony out
and he'd quickly gone to sleep.

On the other hand, watching Zach in nothing but some worn board shorts had nearly short-
circuited her nervous system. She'd been desper-
ate to get him in the pool, so she couldn't see so
much, but then he'd gotten all wet and that hadn't
helped one little bit. Thank goodness they had
Tony to keep them occupied as they tried to keep
him from driving everyone crazy.

She heard his door open and he popped his
head around the door. Tony was still asleep, so she
went over to see what he wanted. A very bad move
on her part, the man had obviously been in the
gym. He was hot and sweaty, and she wanted to...
well she wanted to do too many things to count.

He whispered, "Do you want to order room service or go out for breakfast?"

"I think Tony's heart is set on some of those pastries from Emma's."

Zach grinned. "They did look good. I'll get showered then. How much longer do you think he'll sleep?"

"Not long. I'm a little surprised he's not up already, the pool really tuckered him out."

"That and the sand dunes, and the trip in general. Being that excited all the time should require some down time to compensate."

Emma nodded. "He is a little high strung."

Zach shrugged. "He's five."

"Yeah and he'll be hopping from foot to foot talking about starving before you get out of the shower, so move it."

He chuckled. "Yes, ma'am."

Emma breathed a sigh of relief as she went back into her room. Two more minutes with him and she wouldn't be held accountable for her actions. She was holding on by a thread of willpower from jumping the man. She wasn't sure how much longer she'd be able to hold out with spending so much time with him. For goodness sake, he was dripping with sweat and even stunk, but she still wanted him like crazy. She was obviously a certifiable nutcase. His sweaty self hadn't turned her off and his odor was even pleasant to her nostrils.

She sat in the chair in the room and tried to think of anything but the thought of Zach naked in the shower, hot water sluicing over his body. She held in a groan and willed Tony to wake up, but he was still fast asleep.

Work, she should think about work. She pulled up her email on her phone to see if anyone needed anything. She was both pleased and frustrated that there wasn't one single email she needed to handle. Pleased that her clients were doing fine. Frustrated that there was nothing to think about to contain her wayward thoughts of Zach.

She checked Facebook, nothing.

She checked Instagram, nothing.

She checked Twitter, nothing.

She even went to her Pinterest account, and couldn't find anything interesting to take her mind off the man in the next room.

Finally, Tony woke up, thank God, and she busily helped him get ready for the day. Tony kept telling her he could get dressed on his own, but she didn't back off. Zach walked in all clean and damp just as she got Tony in his shoes.

Tony jumped off the bed and ran to give Zach a hug. "Mama must be awful hungry because she helped me get dressed. I don't really need help.

I aaamm five years old."

Zach ruffled his son's hair then winked at Emma. "Well, *I'm* hungry. So, I'm not going to complain about your mom helping you, even if you are five and perfectly capable of getting dressed. Let's head out. Some darn fine-looking pastries are calling my name."

"Yay! I think they're calling my name too, Daddy Z."

"Get your coat on, pardner, it's probably pretty chilly out this morning."

Emma did one last skim of the room and bathroom, to make sure they hadn't left anything behind, as Zach and Tony took everything to the truck. Then she slowly followed them, giving herself a little time to cool down before she spent the next twelve hours in close quarters with Zach.

Tony was trying to help Zach carry their things to the car and largely just getting in the way, but Zach didn't want to discourage him. It was good that kids wanted to help and emulate people older than they were. In this day and age of electronics it seemed like kids became enthralled with their games and movies, and left the real world behind. Which was part of the reason Zach had bought a bunch of things for Tony to do that were not electronics. He'd bought plenty of both, actually, but was pleased when Tony had opted for the coloring books, and the map, and playing twenty questions and I Spy with them.

Tony asked, "Are we staying in a hotel again tonight?"

"Yes. And then tomorrow we should get to my sister's by lunch time or maybe a little after that."

"Can we get another hotel that has a swimming pool. I love the swimming pool."

Zach laughed, that was an understatement. "We can try."

"Okay. If we can't get one maybe we could do some coloring, or play one of the games you got me, or read stories. But I would love to go swimming again, the very best. Maybe mama could find us another hotel, she's very good on her phone."

Zach ruffled Tony's hair. "She is, indeed. But first we need to have breakfast, don't you think?"

Tony jumped up and down. "Are we going back to Emma's restaurant? They had some mighty yummy looking breakfast foods."

"Yes, we are, here comes your mom so hop up into your car seat."

"It's a booster seat Daddy Z, I graduated out of a car seat."

"All right, then hop up into your booster seat."

Emma called out. "Did you check us out already?"

"Yes."

"But I was going to pay my half."

"Nope."

"Zach..."

"Emma, we're on the way to see my mom and sister. I will pay for the trip."

"But..."

"No buts, let's roll, Tony is hungry."

She shook her finger at him. "Fine, but this conversation isn't over."

"Yes, it is." He grabbed that finger and kissed it. They both froze, and their gazes locked.

Emma broke the staring match first. "Kissing is not going to deter me."

Zach harrumphed. "We'll see about that." As he walked to his side of the truck he muttered, "Maybe kissing more than her finger will deter her. Sure would be worth it to experiment."

When he climbed in the truck, she said, "I saw you muttering all the way around the truck. What were you saying?"

He looked at her with a purely wicked expression. "Do you really want to discuss this now?" He nodded his head toward Tony.

She glanced at her son, then turned bright red. "Um, no, I guess not."

He didn't dare grin, but he wanted to. In fact, he wanted to crow with delight, he was getting to her. Little by little, and he couldn't be happier about that.

Chapter 16

When they got to the café, one of the servers walked up to Tony and crouched down. "Are you Tony?"

Tony looked confused but said, "Yes I am."

"Good. We've been saving you the best table and some of the best breakfast foods we sell. Our special pastries sell out very quickly in the morning, but we put some aside for you and your family."

"Why did you do that? How did you know I was Tony?"

The woman started leading them to a table. "The waitresses from last night told me all about you and how excited you were to come in this morning."

"They did? All of them were very nice to me last night." He looked around and lowered his voice. "They even gave me ice cream we didn't order."

"Well, my oh my, they only give ice cream to their very favorite people. You must be one of them. Now I think they told me that you like Aquaman, is that right?"

Tony hopped up and down before climbing into his chair. "I do love Aquaman. Mama is letting me grow my hair longer, so we match."

"That's nice of your mama to do that."

"She's a good mama."

Emma didn't know what to say about all the preferential treatment they were giving Tony, she looked up at Zach and he just shrugged, so she decided to let it go for now.

The waitress turned to them. "No need to order, we're just going to bring you out a sampling of everything. We'll just charge you for two adult meals and one child's, so no worries. If you want something different after we bring out what we saved for the little guy, you can order then."

Zach and Emma both nodded, neither of them knowing what to say.

Tony's eyes got huge when the staff started putting the food on the table. Not only had they saved him some of their special treats, but they'd taken the time and effort to make them look like elements from Aquaman.

There was a trident shaped sopapilla, cheese and mango Danishes shaped like fish, pancakes that looked like dolphins, an omelet that was vaguely shaped like a chest with golden circles of ham, and the crepe they brought out was amazing. It actually looked very much like a seahorse. How they'd managed that she had no idea. There was enough food for ten people, but it all looked amazing and Tony was in awe.

Emma took pictures of the table with the whole spread and then a closeup of each individual dish, before they dug in. Everything was delicious.

Emma asked the waitress which items would be the best to take with them in a doggy bag for later. Everything was best fresh, but she understood that they couldn't eat it all and Tony would want to take the leftovers with him. They bagged up what was left of the most easily transportable items and Emma encouraged the guys to eat the others.

When they were stuffed to the gills, ha ha, they managed to pay and waddle out to the truck. Tony had given each waitress a hug goodbye and had insisted on giving the cook and bus help, one too.

Emma knew this would be one of his fondest memories of childhood and she cherished how these strangers had worked hard to give her son something special to remember for the rest of his life. She thought about making a picture book of the trip.

She'd met Jeremy Scott the children's book author when he'd come from Chelan for Alyssa's wedding. She wondered if it would be too rude to ask him about it. Alyssa would know, she made a mental note to ask her and decided she would document the trip a little more as they went.

∞∞∞∞

Zach was shocked at the way they had been treated, he recognized that Tony was a bright and appealing child, but he hadn't counted on others thinking so, too. Family and friends seemed normal, but these complete strangers had surprised the heck out of him. They'd barely let him pay anything for their breakfast fit for a king, or should he say the king of the oceans.

Tony gushed, "That was so much fun, can we come back here again?"

"Not this trip, but maybe someday," Zach said with a shake of his head.

"I've never eaten food that was so fun. It was yummy, too. I'm going to color in my Aquaman coloring book, now."

Zach glanced at Emma. "That was not something I've ever experienced."

She shook her head. "Neither have I. I'm not

quite sure what to think of it all. Other than I think it will be a memory that lasts a lifetime for him."

Zach nodded. "Me too. It was awful nice of them to go to so much trouble."

"It was. They are good people. Both the night shift and the day shift. The owners must be exceptional. You don't have a crew that wonderful unless they are happy in their work."

"Yep. I wonder if one of them was the owner."

Emma gasped. "That never even occurred to me."

"I said something about them getting into trouble for charging us so little and giving us so much food. The lady told me not to worry about that, and then she winked at me."

"Oh! I'll bet one of them was the owner then. Do you think it was one from this morning or one from last night?"

"No idea."

Emma sighed. "It was definitely a special day. I think we have enough food left over for lunch, or at least a generous snack."

"That was quick thinking, to find out what would keep the best. and putting it away."

"I'm a mom, we have to be quick thinkers

to outwit the little ones and the people they wrap around those tiny fingers of theirs. When we get to your sister's house, you'll have to be the one to run interference."

"Oh lord, I hadn't thought about that. But you're right. I need to cowboy up!"

She laughed. "I'm sure you can handle it, big bad rodeo star that you are."

He tried to be nonchalant, when her laugh had just shimmered through him. The woman had a laugh that really got to him. "I'll do my best."

"Since we ate enough breakfast for six people, we can probably go ahead and drive on through to your next spot, and make up the hour or so we lost yesterday, after the trip to the sand dunes."

"Yeah maybe, we'll see how it goes. I was thinking of Albuquerque."

Emma pulled out her phone and after a few taps said, "Only four hours. I think that will work. We can always stop for a potty break and to stretch our legs if we need to."

"Tony asked me if we could find another hotel with a swimming pool. I told him we could try, and he assured me that you would be able to find one, because you were very good on your phone."

Emma groaned. "That sounds like a gauntlet I'm going to have to pick up."

"Yeah. I was thinking Las Cruces."

"Fine I'll see what I can find."

"It's a big enough city I think you'll be fine, plus it's early in the season so unless there is a conference or concert going on it shouldn't be hard to book." He laughed. "I did have to sleep in my truck one night there, there was a concert and two conferences going on, after checking a bunch of hotels I just gave up and slept in my truck. Fortunately, by that time I had this one, but it still wasn't pleasant."

Emma grimaced. "Let's hope that doesn't happen again."

Zach turned up the radio while Emma searched for a hotel and Tony colored. He was content to drive down the road with his little family. He wished they could be a little family, full time. He imagined pulling the horse trailer on the way to a rodeo with Emma by his side and Tony in the back seat with maybe a little sister. He loved the idea. It felt perfect. Whether Tony or Emma would feel that way he had no idea.

But a man could wish and maybe throw up a prayer or two.

Chapter 17

Emma did find a hotel with a pool and an indoor water slide and Tony had been thrilled. They'd settled into an easy rhythm, stopping when they needed to. Playing games when Tony got bored. She and Zach chatting while their son took a nap. Emma had to admit she could get used to this.

She knew that the road was not always easy and sometimes it was just plain hard, but so far on this trip she'd loved every minute of it, and she was glad she'd suggested they bring Tony to meet the other half of his family. She wondered if she should mention to Zach maybe changing Tony's last name to his. It was something to think about, maybe on down the line.

They'd driven in two four hour shifts today and it hadn't been any harder on Tony to do so. He seemed to be quite content with his box full of diversions, that Zach had supplied. She wondered where Zach had gotten the idea for the storage caddy that sat in the back seat next to Tony, filled with all kinds of wonders, that they could then simply carry into the hotel for the night.

After the swimming pool Tony wasn't quite ready for bed and he'd convinced Zach to color with him for a while. It hadn't taken a lot of convincing, Zach seemed to be happy to spend the time with his son.

Emma had used the time to check email and make sure there weren't any issues she needed to deal with. She'd had two questions, but both were easy, so she answered them quickly. Then she sent her mom a text telling her they were having fun and had included some of the pictures from breakfast and the Great Sand Dunes. They'd texted back and forth for a while.

When she was finished on her phone, she noticed Tony was starting to fade and was getting a little grumpy. "Time for bed boys, we've got another long drive tomorrow and then lots of excitement as we meet the family."

Tony rubbed his eyes. "I am kinda tired. Can I have one more bite of my fishy before I go to bed?"

"That would be fine, Tony, but then it's time for bed and no arguing."

"I'm too tired to argue, Mama. Thanks for coloring with me, Daddy."

Zach looked both startled and pleased that Tony had left off the Z in what he called him. Emma realized Tony was feeling more comfortable with Zach and the two were growing closer. She just hoped that was a good thing.

She didn't want Tony's heart to break when Zach went back on the road. She knew hers probably would. She wondered for the first time if this was a good idea. She didn't want Tony to be hurt. The question was, how could she avoid it, or at the very least soften the blow? Something to think about. They had a few months before Zach needed to get back on the road, so there was time.

Tony finished with his snack and she sent him to the bathroom to brush his teeth before bed. When he came out, he kissed Zach goodnight and then her, and climbed into his bed. Zach had a rueful grin on his face that tore at her heart. Then he shook his head and it was gone.

He got up and walked across the hall to his own room, bidding her goodnight. They hadn't been able to get adjoining rooms this time. She wasn't completely sure that was a bad thing.

∞∞∞∞

Zach was blown away by Tony calling him Daddy instead of Daddy Z, it seemed so much more personal. Emma had noticed it too and had looked as startled as he'd felt. Such a tiny thing, one single letter, and it made him feel like he went from peripheral family to close family. It was the name Tony would have called him if he'd been around the last five years.

He texted his mom to tell her they were in Albuquerque and were on track to be there by lunchtime tomorrow, and he would let her know if anything came up that changed that. She sent him a gif about being excited. He chuckled and thought back to the conversation they'd had a few days before. He'd never figured out how to tell the story in email, so he finally just bit the bullet and called.

She'd been surprised to hear he wasn't coming back for a few more days. He'd never planned to stay even a week, and this was going on three weeks.

"I thought you would be pulling in about now, Zach. You said you were going to make it a fast trip."

"Funny thing about that, mom. I got some rather astonishing news when I got here."

"Okaaay, so is that why you're calling, instead of driving in?"

"Yes, and it's also the reason I'm going to come get my horses and gear at the end of the week. I'm going to come stay here in Colorado at the Rockin' K."

"But…"

"Yeah, I know. So maybe you should sit down for the rest of this conversation."

"Why, what's wrong? Is one of the Kipling's sick? Dying? Do I need to come help out?"

"No, mom. None of those things. In fact, this could be considered really good news." He took a deep breath and soldiered on, "You know, Emma had a son, that Drew said was illegitimate?"

"Yes, and I'd had such high hopes for the two of you. But you've been stubbornly avoiding Emma and all the Kipling's ever since."

"Right. Well it turns out Emma's son, is really my son, too."

His mother had screeched over the phone, "What?"

"Yeah, so are you sitting down?"

"Zach, just tell me how she got pregnant with your son, and more importantly why you didn't go back and claim your rightful place by her side."

"You know the night before I left, we had the party on the plateau and there was some drinking involved."

"Some? You smelled like a brewery the next morning. I wasn't sure you were completely sober when you drove off."

"Yeah well, that's part of it. I was pretty buzzed, got tired, went into my tent, alone, and fell promptly to sleep. Emma came in a little while later when everyone had called it a night. I was asleep, but she didn't know it."

"Oh no, were you talking in your sleep?"

"Yes, and apparently, we had quite the conversation about me loving her, but wanting to give her time to grow up, and make some life choices. I told her I wasn't going to cross the line from friendship to more until she graduated high school."

He huffed out a breath. "Well according to Emma, she told me it wasn't only my choice to make. That she wanted to make love to me one time before I went off to rodeo, because it was a dangerous sport. She didn't want to run the risk of me not coming back and her having regrets for the rest of her life, by never being with me."

"Oh, no, so you weren't that drunk."

"No. My body happily responded to her kisses and... stuff."

"Didn't she think to use a condom?"

"Yes, she did. She snatched a couple of them from Daniel and Kristine's wedding party. Not knowing Drew and I had poked holes in all of them as a gag gift for Daniel."

His mother groaned. "You've got to be joking. You couldn't script this kind of thing for a soap opera."

"Exactly, but that's how it is that I have a five-year-old son, that I'm bringing to meet you and why I'm taking my horses and gear back to the Rockin' K, so I can spend that time getting to know my child. He's delightful, by the way, and is the spitting image of me at that age."

"You're bringing him here to meet me? But he doesn't know you, why would Emma let you take him this far?"

"Emma's coming too."

"Oh, why didn't Emma tell you about the boy?"

"She told Drew to tell me. She was only seventeen and didn't know how I would react. Probably a little scared in fact. The only problem with that scenario was that all the boys, and especially Adam, had decided she'd been with a tourist who hadn't stayed, so that's what Drew told me."

"But when you didn't show up..."

"She assumed I wanted nothing to do with her or Tony."

His mother huffed. "Well she didn't know you very well, then. Of course, you would have wanted to be a part of his life."

Zach was so damn sad to realize she hadn't known him at all. "That's the real crux of the matter, she *didn't* know me. I don't think we'd ever spent more than one or two minutes alone, ever. Well up until the night Tony was conceived. Before that it had always been a group of us. We were both attracted to the other, but neither one of us had acted on it. Which is why she took matters into her own hands that night, thinking I would remember it and know how she felt. And that I would remember telling her how I much I loved her. Instead I drove off not aware of either."

His mother made a strangled sound. "I don't know whether to laugh at the comedy of errors or cry at what all you missed out on."

"I totally agree. Which is why I am spending the spring at the ranch."

"But first you're bringing them here. I cannot wait to see him." There had been a pause and then she'd continued, "So, that's why you asked me to send that picture of you in the Tarzan shirt."

"Yeah, we look almost identical, except for the eye color. Tony has brown like his mother. Mom, she named him Anthony James."

"Oh Zach, even though you hadn't come back to support her, she still named him after you." He could hear the tears clogging her throat.

"Yeah, she did."

She coughed. "Well you just get here as soon as you can, and we'll have a great time with him.

So… are you and Emma…"

"No, we're being platonic. But she's giving me full access to Tony, holding nothing back."

"Do you want to change things with her? Maybe become a family?"

"On one hand, hell yes. On the other, I don't know her, any more than she knows me. So, I'm taking it slow."

"Good, but not too slow. Or she will either decide you don't want that with her anymore, or she'll take matters into her own hands, and that didn't work out so well last time."

He chuckled. "I don't plan to drink again, maybe ever. And now she knows I talk and do other things in my sleep, so I don't think that scenario is likely to happen again. But I'll keep your words in mind."

"Well, keep me up to date on your arrival, here."

"Will do, love you mom."

"Love you too, Zach. I can't wait to go tell your sister all of this." He could hear the excitement in her voice.

"Better you than me. Have fun."

He wondered what all his mom had done since that conversation. Finding out about a five-year-old grandson was enough to send the woman into a tizzy. Or a buying frenzy... kind of like he'd done. Good grief, between the two of them, they were going to spoil the kid rotten in less than a week.

Zach was kind of bummed out that they hadn't gotten adjoining rooms tonight. He did enjoy Tony running back and forth from room to room. But considering how tired the little guy was, it wasn't likely to happen. Tony had tried to convince them that it would be fine for Zach to stay in the room with him and his mom.

Emma's cheeks had turned red and he'd lost his breath for a moment as his heart had yearned for that. But then he'd told Tony that he didn't want to wake them up with his snoring. He didn't think he really snored, but it was the only thing he could think of.

Tony hadn't really bought that, but then Emma had quickly said that since Tony slept in the middle of the bed like a flattened frog there wasn't room for either her or Zach. Tony had gone off giggling about being a smashed frog and the idea had been dropped, to the great relief of both parents.

Zach had taken note that a ridiculous statement was much more effective for curbing a five-year-old's question than something reasonable. He was learning by leaps and bounds on this trip, about his son, but also about Emma. He wasn't quite sure, which, he cherished more.

Chapter 18

Since Tony had dropped like a stone into sleep last night, he did not sleep late the next morning and was up and raring to go nearly before the sun came up. Emma on the other hand had lain awake for hours thinking about Zach and all she was discovering about him. So, when Tony started hopping up and down on his bed, loudly making himself known, she was not a happy camper.

"Tony, for the love of God, be quiet."

"Sorry, mama, but I get to meet my new grandma and aunt and cousins today and I'm so excited."

"I know, but..." She was interrupted by a text on her phone.

> Zach: Want me to take the little hellion down to the gym and then we'll go get some fast food breakfast? It'll give you another hour.

> Emma: I would happily worship at your feet

for another hour.

Zach: LOL No worship needed. Tell him to get dressed and I'll be there in ten minutes.

Emma: Yay!

"Tony, get dressed. Zach is going to come get you in five minutes, to do some manly stuff and then get breakfast."

"Yay!"

He grabbed his clean outfit and Emma said, "No, wear yesterday's clothes, so you don't get your meeting people outfit all dirty."

"Okay, mama. Clean underwear and socks? Or dirty ones?"

"Clean underwear and socks. If you get too dirty you can change those again when you change your clothes. And brush your teeth."

"Yes, mama."

When Tony came out of the bathroom ready to go, she was shocked to see he'd even combed his hair and washed his face and hands. Her baby was growing up. She threw on a robe and opened the door to find Zach there in gym clothes with his hand raised to knock. He grinned at her as Tony rushed to give him a hug around his knees.

Zach took one look at her in her pjs and then said, "You take your time. I've got the squirt."

She yawned. "Bless you, Zach McCoy, bless

you."

Emma heard him chuckle as he led their son down the hall. But she was perfectly happy to flop back in the bed. She was going to take no less than another half hour to sleep, or if not sleep at least rest with her eyes closed.

She awoke to knocking and wondered if Tony had forgotten something. She hurried to the door to find a sweaty man and little boy carrying a fast food breakfast that smelled like heaven.

"How did you get back so soon? I just laid down to rest for a few more minutes."

"It's been an hour and a half."

"No. Really? I must have passed out. Darn. I wanted to be ready when you got back."

"No need for that, both Tony and I stink, and need a shower. So, after we eat, I'll take him across the hall to get dressed and you can take your time getting ready." He grinned at her. "But no more sleeping."

"We worked out, Mama, just like Aunty S does. It was fun. I lifted weights and everything."

Zach said, "He kept going on and on about how strong Aunty S was. I assume that was Cade's wife, the one that swept the feet out from that guy that was after Lily."

"Yes, Summer, she's in professional cheer-leading and is freakishly strong."

Shirley Penick

Zach's eyebrows rose. "Professional cheer-leading like that movie?"

"*Bring it on*? Yes. She is also the actress that played Heather in the TV show *Training up Heather*."

"Really." I never watched that much but my sister cried buckets of tears when they took it off TV."

"Yes, really."

"Wow a real live TV star in the family. Hey how come we didn't know any of this in high school?"

"She was hiding. It's a long story I'll tell you later on the drive. We need to get finished with breakfast and cleaned up to get on the road if we want to get to your sister's place by lunch time."

"True. You about done eating, Tony?"

"Yep."

"Okay, then grab some clean undies and your clean clothes and let's go get showered."

Tony clapped his hands and jumped up and down. "Yes, sir. I want to get a move on, so we can get there soon."

Emma smiled as the two guys gathered up what Tony needed to get ready. Emma walked into the bathroom to shower and wanted to scream when she looked in the mirror. Her hair looked like something out of a horror movie. Her pajamas were miniscule, and her face still had a pillow indent. She didn't know how Zach had kept a straight face. Hopefully he'd been looking at the tiny pajamas and not her hair or face. Normally she wouldn't want someone ogling her body, today was an exception to that rule.

∞∞∞

Zach started the water for Tony to shower and then stripped out of his clothes and gathered clean ones for the day. He would have joined his son in the shower, but Emma's itty-bitty pajamas had set off raging hormones that he didn't want to have to explain to his five-year-old son.

She was so damn beautiful; her hair had been wild around her face but only emphasized, to him, the right out of bed look. The pillow stripe on her face hadn't deterred his body one tiny bit. He'd wanted to grab her and devour her, but his son watching had at least kept him from acting on his impulses. Not from thinking about them, no sir, nothing could have done that.

He might have to devise a way to get Emma by herself. How he could do that, he had no idea, but maybe he could think of something. He wanted to see if she was the least bit interested in more.

Tony was vibrating with excitement when they finally piled into the truck, and Zach was worried this might be where he began the 'Are we there yet?' portion of the trip. He'd not said it even once since they'd left the Rockin' K, but he'd also known it would take two and a half days to get there. Now that they were down to the last half day and in reality, only a handful of hours the impatience might settle in.

After Zach had started the truck, Emma said, "Tony? Can you see the clock up here on the dashboard?"

"I can, if I lean way over."

"Good. Whenever you wonder if we are almost there, I want you to do that and look at the clock. When it says 1-2-3-4, then it will mean we are almost there."

"Okay, Mama. I will look at the clock when I get 'mpatient."

"Great idea."

Zach heaved a sigh of relief; Emma had also anticipated Tony's excitement and had found a way to—if not entirely defuse it—at least to postpone it. He reached over and squeezed her hand. She looked up and he grinned at her in appreciation for her quick thinking. She smiled back which caused a distinct flutter in the region of his heart.

He would have been happy to hold her hand for the next four hours, but he loosened his grip and she put her hand back in her lap. His hand felt lonely without hers in it, and he was sounding like a sap to his own ears. He gave himself a stern talking to about not acting like a dumbass. He didn't think it was going to help one bit.

Chapter 19

Tony and his cousins raced through the kitchen and out into the backyard. Both Wes and Vern had acceded leadership of their small band to Tony. Both of Natalie's children were much more laid back than Tony had ever been. Zach's mother, Betty, said, "Tony's just like Zach was at that age, full of energy and raring to go."

Emma and Betty were sitting at the worn kitchen table with mugs of hot coffee in their hands. The kitchen was a cozy place and clearly the center of the household where everyone gathered to chat. There were little statues of pigs on every surface, along with all kinds of kitschy pig décor, towels, napkin holders, curtains, salt and pepper shakers, you name it and there was a pig on it. Someone clearly loved pigs.

Emma tore her eyes away from the pigs, she wanted to count them. "I wondered. Since I was the youngest, I wasn't sure whether he'd gotten it from Zach or one of my brothers. Cade was a possibility since he's never met a stranger, but I couldn't imagine the others being quite so rambunctious. Maybe mom just chased them out in the yard when they got wild."

Betty laughed. "Oh, I'm sure they all had their moments. I can't imagine five boys not butting heads on occasion."

"Absolutely. I do remember mom chasing them out of the house with a broom, one time. Telling them to go outside and fight. If I recall correctly it was freezing cold and sleeting. The fight didn't last long, they were too cold out in that weather, in stockinged feet and no coats."

"Meg is a very intelligent woman."

"That she is. Tony doesn't have anyone to fight with, yet. But mom's still given me many good ideas on how to handle Tony. Fortunately, Tony's personality leans toward exuberance and not fighting."

"So, tell me, Emma, why didn't you call Zach back when you found yourself with child?"

Emma stiffened, she knew this conversation would take place at some time, but she still didn't like it. "Well first I didn't have his phone number and didn't want to ask for it. Plus, I honestly thought I had. I told Drew to tell him I was pregnant and due in November. I had no idea the stupid thought of me sleeping with some stranger was being believed. It was so farfetched, I was sure they'd been teasing me, although it did hurt my feelings for them to be saying it, so I didn't discuss it with them. When Zach didn't come home right away, I figured he was finishing up his rodeo commitments and would be back in the fall or winter."

Emma took a deep breath and soldiered on. "When he wasn't there for Tony's birth, I assumed he didn't want anything to do with us, or had a new girlfriend or something. I didn't want to out him with my family, so I didn't give Tony his last name, but I did give him James as a middle name."

Betty's eyes filled with tears. "My husband would have been so proud, that you gave Tony his name as the middle name. What did Zach say when he heard?"

Emma smiled a sad smile. "Something about my brother's being clueless not to recognize it. Anyway, when my stupid brothers perpetuated the ridiculous idea that Tony was some drifter's kid, I didn't argue, mostly because I was too heartbroken that Zach hadn't wanted me and his son, so I really didn't care what they said."

"Oh, honey, he would never have left you like that if he'd known."

"But I didn't know that. I'd just barely turned eighteen, when Tony was born, so I didn't have a lot of confidence. But my family was kind and caring and never made me feel bad about having Tony without a husband. I gained a lot by having him."

Emma sat up straight and squared her shoulders. "So, I enrolled in online college, studying when Tony slept. I eventually got a couple of accounting clients, and built my business slowly. I will graduate in May and I'm very excited about that."

Betty took her hand and squeezed it much like Zach did on occasion. "You should be very proud of yourself. You've done a good job raising Tony and building a business and getting your degree. You are a remarkable young woman."

"So, you aren't mad at me for missing out on Tony's life because I was a chicken?"

"Mad? Absolutely not. A little heartbroken for myself, but even more for Zach. He missed out on a special time of life with his first-born son."

Emma nearly gasped at the idea of Zach having other children. She'd never thought of him getting married and having other little ones. The idea hurt so bad; she almost couldn't breathe. She needed a moment to herself.

She stood and said, "I brought Tony's baby book, and some other photo albums. I'll go get them, so you can look through them. I'll be right back."

Emma fled to the room she'd been given,

and nearly fell to her knees, as she gave into the pain of Zach marrying. But she had to admit to herself that he was still young and might want more kids. She had to steel her heart against this pain. She had to be strong for Tony, who would end up being a stepchild and never quite part of the family. But he was always going to be the most important to her, and her whole family loved him in every way.

She got up off the bed and went to her bag of albums she'd brought and took them into where Betty was still seated at the kitchen table. Forcing a bright smile, she laid the books down for Betty to enjoy.

∞∞∞

Zach was giving each of his horses a thorough ride. They would be in the trailer for a couple of days straight with only the evenings out, so he wanted to make sure all four of them were stretched and healthy.

Once that was done, he was going to clean the trailer both in the horse section and also in the living quarters. He didn't think the living quarters was too messy or dirty, but it never hurt to give everything a good cleaning and wash anything that needed it, sheets, towels, and the like. He hoped that Emma and Tony would want to sleep in the trailer on the drive back. They could take the queen bed and he could sleep on the fold out sofa.

The last day before they left, he'd give his horses another run, maybe Emma would like to help him. None of his horses would work for Tony, they were trained for speed not children. Zach knew Alex had one or two his kids could ride, so maybe he could borrow one and they could all go. He'd not seen Tony on a horse yet, but he was certain he'd been taught to ride.

Zach was just bringing in his last horse when he saw the three boys with ropes practicing with a team roping dummy. It looked like they were taking turns, one pulling the calf, one heading and one heeling. Tony had pulled the last time and it looked like he was moving to heeling.

Zach slowly walked his horse to the barn as he watched. His chest puffed out with pride as Tony expertly roped the calf's back two legs. Damned if Tony wasn't a mighty fine roper already at the age of five. Of course, Cade had practically been a legend in Colorado with his rope before that crazy girlfriend of his had made him quit rodeoing.

As Tony moved to the header position, Zach stopped his horse to watch. As far as Zach could tell Tony did everything exactly correct, even his form was excellent, and his rope didn't wobble.

Emma walked out of the back door and over to where Zach was on his horse. She looked so pretty, only somehow kind of sad, but before he could hardly register that, she smiled so big he thought his heart might explode from the sight of it. "Tony does pretty well for a little guy, don't you think?"

Zach raised his eyebrows. "Pretty well? I think he's doing a damn fine job. I didn't know Cade was working with him that much, but it sure shows."

Emma huffed. "Cade has worked with him some, for sure, but I've done most of it."

Zach turned his head back slowly from where it had drifted back to the boys and met Emma's eyes. "You've been working with him? Really? I remember you were roping well with Cade before that woman talked him out of participating. I didn't know you'd kept up with it."

"Whenever I have time I go out and catch me a few cattle. Since I was the header, I don't need a heeler to practice. Then after a while, I go out and startle a few calves to make them run and capture their feet."

Emma shrugged. "No one really knew I was doing it. I just snuck it in when I had the time for a ride. Even took Chika out and ran some barrels, but the poor thing is getting too old. She still loves it, so I take her out and let her run them every week or two. We take it pretty easy though."

Zach was surprised that Emma had been keeping up with her roping and barrel riding, he wouldn't call it racing, now that her horse was getting up there in years. He didn't figure Emma had a lot of spare time, so to take her rope and work out with it was a little bit of a surprise. "Well when we get back to the ranch you can show me your skills. I can be your heeler."

Her eyes sparkled with excitement. "Maybe I want to be the heeler."

He laughed. "As you wish. But I'm better at heeling."

"Speaking of which. Where is your real header? I know you were doing well in the event last year." Her eyes widened, and she slapped a hand over her mouth.

His heart nearly exploded with joy. He got down off his horse and got up close to Emma. "So, you've been watching the stats, have you? And maybe some of the streaming."

"I admit to nothing."

"You already did, darlin'." He wanted to kiss her so damn bad, just two or three inches separated them, but he wasn't sure she was ready for it, so he eased back, rather than forward. She looked at his lips and licked her own, he nearly groaned.

He wanted her to be sure of them, so he

eased back a little more. "To answer your question, he swapped out to another partner. I haven't found a new one yet, so I was considering just doing the one event until I can find another partner for team roping."

"Oh."

He didn't think she'd even heard what he'd said.

She frowned, grabbed him by the shirt and pulled him down for a kiss. He didn't have to be told twice and kissed her with a hunger he'd not known was even there. She tasted like heaven and sin, all rolled into one. Her lips soft, her mouth open, and her tongue dueling with his. His brain short circuited and all he could do was keep up.

His body burned with passion for her and he buried his hands in her hair. They might have stayed there all day, if one of the kids hadn't whooped and his horse hadn't nudged him. They broke apart panting.

She looked over the top of his saddle to where the children were.

Zach laid one hand on his horse. "I better go groom this guy; I gave him a hard run."

"Yeah, I better go see what the kids are up to."

Zach nodded then met her direct gaze. "But this isn't over."

"No, it sure as hell is not, Zach, and I'll have no excuses this time." Then she turned on her heel and walked over to the kids.

Excuses? This time? Did she mean what he thought she meant? His body sure thought so. Hot damn, he better get his trailer cleaned out. It might make a perfect rendezvous location.

Chapter 20

Emma didn't know whether to be mortified or bold as hell with Zach. She'd practically propositioned the man in the yard, in front of three kids, and who knew how many onlookers. His pupils had dilated so she knew he'd gotten her meaning, but then he'd disappeared for the rest of the day and she didn't know what to make of it.

She'd decided that if she didn't want Zach married and having kids with some other woman, then maybe she should let him know she was still interested. So, when he'd looked like he wanted to kiss her, she'd seized the reins, and Zach.

They'd just all sat down for dinner when Zach rushed in still damp from a shower. "Sorry I'm late. I didn't want to stink up the place. Wanted to get the trailer cleaned up for the drive."

He'd been cleaning the trailer, after her display in the yard? Well that didn't bode too well. Maybe he'd been glad to get away from her. No. He'd been enthusiastic in his response to her kiss and had amped up the heat.

Emma wasn't going to think negatively; she'd wait and see. He'd said it wasn't over. Yeah, she needed to be patient. She wasn't seventeen anymore, they would be near each other for the next six to eight weeks, no reason to panic.

When everyone had filled their plates and began eating, Zach's mother put her fork down. "I want to take the kids to see Francine tomorrow."

Alex asked, "All of them?"

At the same time Natalie said, "To Mesa? But it's a two-hour drive. Francine usually comes here."

"I am capable of driving for two hours. Francine can't get away this week. And yes, all of them, she's never met Tony and he's having too much fun with his cousins to separate them." She looked at Zach. "No comment?"

"Nope. Are you going to stay overnight?"

"That was my idea, that way no one gets too tired. I decided all the parents could use a day off."

Natalie and Alex exchanged a look and then nodded. "Fine with us."

Zach said, "Me too. Emma, what do you think?"

Emma looked around the table and saw confident expressions on each face. Wes and Vern's eyes had lit up, so it looked to her that Francine was a favorite. "Tony do you want to go on another drive to meet one of your grandma's friends?"

Tony looked at his cousins who were nodding enthusiastically. "Sure, mama. Are you going to stay here?"

Emma and Tony had never been separated for that long, but he was getting older and it was only two hours. If they needed to, they could drive up and get him. "Yes, I'll stay here, and you can have a grand adventure with your grandmother and cousins."

He nodded and grinned at his cousins.

Her heart clutched for a second, her little boy was growing up, but she said, "Then it's fine with me, too."

Betty grinned. "Excellent, we'll leave at nine in the morning."

Emma glimpsed an odd expression on Zach's face, but it only lasted a moment, so she wasn't sure what it meant.

Wes and Vern happily entertained Tony with stories of Nanny Francine, while they ate their dinner. By the time dinner was finished Tony was vibrating with excitement to go meet this practically perfect woman, the way the boys had described her made Mary Poppins sound like a slouch. She hoped he would be able to sleep to-night, but he'd had a busy day playing with his cousins, so she hadn't needed to worry.

The three boys took a bath together, splashing and making a god-awful mess. She'd decided to let Zach supervise bathtime, while she packed Tony a backpack to take with him with two changes of clothes, just in case, and a few things the boys could play with together in the car.

When Zach brought Tony into her room, he was drenched. Zach's shirt clung to his body, molded to every muscle. His jeans were soaked. It made her want to strip him down and dry him off, slowly and with great care. Instead, she laughed at his sardonic expression. "So, you got a second shower."

"Yeah, but Alex is wetter than I am, he's got two boys gunning for him."

Tony yawned. "I'm getting kinda tired mommy, can we have a quick story, tonight?"

"Sure, sweetheart, get your pjs on and hop into bed."

Zach looked down at himself. "I'll forego story time, so the bed doesn't get wet. See you both in the morning."

"Night, Daddy."

"Night, Son." Zach kissed his son on the top of his head and walked out the door.

Emma was nearly overcome by that simple exchange, so she waved to Zach when he turned back, and went to help Tony get ready for bed.

As she read the story to her sweet son, she grieved for what might have been. If only she'd been brave enough to call Zach herself and tell him about Tony, how much their lives might have changed. She vowed never again to be afraid to stand up for what she wanted. To boldly speak out the truth, whether it scared her to do so or not. She'd been a fool to leave something so important in someone else's hand.

She was determined to lock that fearful Emma into a closet, and never let her make stupid choices based on anxiety again.

∞∞∞∞

Zach was fairly certain his mother was removing Tony from the equation to give him some time alone with Emma. He was doubly glad he'd cleaned out the trailer this afternoon. He'd put clean sheets on the bed and fresh towels in the bathroom, and stuck the dirty ones in the washer. He needed to put them into the dryer, so he could fold them up and bring them along.

He quickly detoured to do just that and then went to his room to strip out of the wet clothes. Three boys having a hilarious time in a bathtub was an insane experience. Tony all by himself was bad enough, but add in two more... completely out of control.

He grinned, hysterically funny though, he couldn't deny it. What one didn't think of the other two did. Since he and Alex had laughed at their antics early on, the boys had tried more and more silliness to get their fathers to laugh again.

A lesson to be learned for later he supposed. Sometimes a parent couldn't allow themselves to laugh, there were times where it wouldn't be appropriate, and maybe even times where it might be dangerous for a child to act out. Yeah, he wanted to remember this for the future.

Speaking of the future, he needed to think about how to get Emma alone tomorrow, so he could start his campaign to woo her back to him, and away from the good doctor. He'd not seen her talk to him again, but that didn't mean she hadn't called him after they had all gone their separate ways at night.

Her grabbing him and kissing the stuffing out of him didn't bode well for poor Ian. And her remark earlier still had him wondering what she was planning. He just hoped it was what he thought she'd meant and not something else entirely.

He hung his wet clothes over some hangers in his half empty closet. A lot of his belongings were in the trailer. Earlier, he'd made sure the built-in wardrobes had enough room for Emma and Tony to put their things in the camper. The suitcases could go in the truck bed, along with supplies for the horses.

He pulled on some dry skivvies and got into bed. He didn't think his mind was going to let him get to sleep too quickly. It was going over so many ideas and desires and plots and plans. Sometimes he wished it came with an off button. He turned the lights off and laid in the dark letting his mind roam.

Images of Emma filled his thoughts. He really didn't want to fight them, so he let her join him in his dreams.

Chapter 21

The kids were loaded into the cars, with all the noise and exuberance Emma had expected. She'd kissed Tony a half dozen times. He was plenty happy with his adventure and she was fairly certain she was going to be a wreck the whole time he was gone.

As they drove down the driveway away from the house and her, she looked around feeling a little crazy. Distraction, she needed a distraction.

She grabbed Zach's arm. "You gotta do something."

His expression turned startled when he looked at her, her eyes were probably wild and panicked looking.

Being the good cowboy, he was, he started talking to her in soothing tones and took her hand. She had no idea where they were headed or what he was even saying, but she went along.

He walked toward the barn, maybe they could go riding. No with her in the state she was in, it wouldn't be good for the horses. Not good to ride when a person, her, was feeling crazed.

Zach led her behind the barn and his words finally penetrated. "...had it about a year and would like a female's perspective. It's worked for me, but it never hurts to think bigger, which is why I bought the one I did, plenty of room for growth."

As they turned the corner, Emma stopped dead in her tracks. In front of her was the biggest, fanciest, horse trailer and camper she'd ever seen. She gaped at Zach. "You, a single guy, bought that? Seriously?

"Well, yeah. My old one was on its last legs and I'd just bought another horse. I'd had a couple of good years and had the money, well most of it..."

Emma doubled up with laughter. "It's huge... Drew is so going to tease you... well maybe not Drew... but for sure Cade..."

"But I live in it nearly twelve months a year. I didn't want to be cramped. And neither did my horses." Zach was frowning with his arms crossed, looking so much like Tony she started laughing again.

"I'm sure... it's wonderful... give me the grand tour."

"Not if you're going to laugh hysterically the whole time."

She forced a straight face. "I wouldn't dream of it."

His mouth twitched, and the tiniest smile started. She let her lips curve into a small smile and his grew, too.

"All right, I admit it is too big for one person. But I think it will be perfect for the drive back to the Rockin' K."

"Well you'll have to prove that. Show me your travelling apartment, cowboy."

He swept his invisible hat off his head and drawled, "After you, ma'am."

Emma went to the back where the horses would be and went inside the tack room. Everything was very efficiently stored. Whoever had designed it really knew what a cowboy on the road six to twelve months a year would need. The horse stalls were angled, and she counted six of them.

"Do you have six horses?"

"No, only four, but I don't plan to buy a new one of these any time soon, so I wanted expansion room."

She could imagine her horse and one for Tony in the last two stalls, but she didn't mention that to Zach and stuffed the idea away into a dark closet.

"This is really nice and well planned. I can't imagine anything better."

"Yeah, I went top of the line. It cost more, but I figured it was worth it."

She walked out the door and around to the other side to see PVC pipe sections attached above the wheel wells. "Is that a portable corral?"

"It is, and it works like a charm. I've got enough pieces to give each horse a decent-sized corral or I can make it into two larger ones. The flexibility is amazing, and the horses love it. Gives them room to move and rest, after being in the trailer all day."

"Happy horses work better."

∞ ∞ ∞

Zach followed Emma into the living quarters where she looked in every cubby hole and cupboard. She examined the bathroom and looked in the fridge. She ran her hands over the counter tops and turned on the water in the sink. She sat on the couch and the corner chair by the door.

Emma looked closely at the couch area and ran a hand down the wall seam. "It looks like this section might pop out."

"Very clever. It does. I've not ever needed to pop it out, but it gives more room in this main area if it's needed."

"And the couch is a fold out."

She'd not even glanced at the queen-sized bed above where the trailer would attach to the truck. "It is, so it could sleep four. If I popped out the side and had a blow-up mattress. I think six might even fit. Certainly, five would, with a single."

She turned toward him and got in close. "Show me the bed, Zach."

He choked and squeaked. "Emma." Zach cleared his throat. "Emma, are you sure about this?"

"I am. I want at least one, wide awake, know what you're doing, sexual encounter in my life, Zach, and you owe me one."

At first his thoughts had jumped to her saying she'd not been with another man. But that was a ridiculous idea. Emma was a beautiful woman, certainly someone had found her irresistible. Maybe even the doctor. He didn't want to think about her with Ian, so he shut down his brain.

"Emma, I would be more than happy to make love to you. I don't think I have any protection anywhere in here."

"Don't you worry your pretty little head

about that. I bought some brand-new ones, without holes poked in them. I've got a couple in my back pocket just in case the opportunity presented itself. So, before I start thinking about why the chance has arrived, and start freaking out again... Show me the bed, Zach."

Zach swallowed. He'd wanted Emma in his bed for so many years he wasn't quite sure how to proceed. He pulled her in close and ran his hands into her hair, pulling the warm silk through his fingers, as he lowered his head to allow his lips access to hers.

She raised up on her toes and met him halfway, he brushed his lips over hers in a soft, almost kiss. Lightning raced through his body from that miniscule contact. And he craved, yearned for more, she apparently felt the same, because her hand went around his neck and she pulled him closer.

He firmed the kiss and pressed his hungry mouth to hers; she moaned in the back of her throat and opened her mouth. He needed no further invitation and his tongue swept inside hers. To taste, to savor, the essence of Emma. She tasted like heaven.

They kissed for long moments as passion grew, their tongues dueling and their bodies pressing closer, wanting more. When they needed air, he broke the kiss and moved his lips to her neck to trace its path from shoulder to ear, where he nibbled. Emma tilted her head to give him better access, and squirmed when he reached her ear. So, he sucked her earlobe into his mouth and her arms tightened around him like a python.

Emma murmured, "This isn't the bed."

He chuckled, "We'll get there, darlin', we have all day and part of tomorrow."

She rubbed up against him and it made his eyes cross with lust. "I'm hoping we'll need to go back into the house later for more condoms, I only brought four."

He barked out a laugh, "You must think I have a lot of stamina."

She rubbed against him again. "I'm counting on it, cowboy."

Whoa, he had his work cut out for him. But he had no intention of disappointing the lady. The first time, though, had to be perfect, so he wasn't going to let her rush him. He wanted to worship every inch of the body he'd dreamt about for years. And in truth had denied he'd wanted the last six years. But that desire had never gone away, he'd lied to himself every morning, telling his mind and heart those weren't dreams about Emma, just some faceless woman.

Well the lying to himself was over and he was going to love this woman so hard that she never thought about another man again. But before he did that, he needed to make sure she wasn't committed to the doctor, he didn't want any misunderstandings later.

"Emma, sweetheart, I'm not trying to break the mood, but do you have anything significant going on with the doctor?"

She looked at him, her eyes clouded with lust and desire. She frowned for a second, then answered, "Ian? No, he's just a client."

"That you brought as your guest to the wedding."

She ducked her head for a moment. "Yeah, I didn't think I could face you without a shield."

Zach thought his heart might soar right out of his body, until she pulled back and looked him in the eye, hers narrowing.

"What about you and Sharon?"

"Yeah that was the stupidest thing I've done, recently anyway. But if you must know when I first danced with her it was to get away from all the bawling women. Still not a wise choice."

"Why were the women crying?"

"Well, let's see, the ones from Montana, something about Lily's friend and the beauty pageant, I'm still not quite sure on that one. The ones from here were that bunch of friends of Monica's, so happy Drew had found someone new."

Emma had a smirk on her face, he wanted to lick it off. "So, you danced with Sharon..."

"Because I knew she didn't give a damn about anyone except herself and there would be no bawling. Unfortunately, I forgot about the even deadlier power of cling."

Emma huffed. "Cling?"

"Yeah like an octopus that you can't get away from. I swear that woman has no less than eight hands and she's fast with them. I felt violated right out there on the dance floor. But you were with Ian and I knew we couldn't talk about Tony at the wedding anyway, so I had to do something. It was either drinking, dancing with the waterworks brigade, or Sharon. I figured Sharon was the best choice."

"I'm not sure I agree with you on that, but..."

"Just so you know. I drove Drew and Lily out to the cabin and then stayed hidden until Sharon gave up and went home with some guy from Montana." He shook his head. "Poor guy."

Emma chuckled. "Yeah, but he lives far enough away not to have to deal with her."

"There is that, but now that we've confessed all, let's get back to me showing you the bed."

"Excellent idea. It would probably be easier to leave the clothes down here, where there's more room."

Zach's body was perfectly happy with that idea. "I can't argue with that. But I want to undress you slowly and enjoy every bit of skin I reveal. Is that acceptable?"

Emma fanned her face with her hand and her eyes heated. "Enjoy away. Maybe I'll take my turn doing the same with you, later."

He sent her a slow, sexy smile. "Happy to oblige, but my turn first, I've been dreaming about it longer than you have."

"I'm not completely sure that's true, but since I had my way with you six years ago, I reckon it's your turn. Enough with the talking, Zach. I think your mouth could be put to much better use."

He pulled back and did a slow perusal of her body, then he licked his lips and grinned. "Yes, ma'am it sure can."

Chapter 22

Emma shivered from the look in Zach's eyes. Oh yeah, she was more than happy to let the cowboy have his way with her. She'd dreamt about it, not that she was going to admit that. At least not right away.

He pulled her back in close and devoured her mouth again. Her body erupting with joy and desire as he did so. This time was a little different, there was no hesitancy. He pulled her in and ran his hands over her curves while his mouth plundered.

Zach's hands found her hips and butt. He squeezed her ass and drew her in closer where she could feel his erection straining to be free. She brushed against him and he groaned in pleasure.

His mouth released hers and went back to her neck. Kissing and licking and nibbling, sending tiny tornados of fire winging through her body, igniting nerve endings as they went spinning toward her core. All those tornados gathered together, and she felt her body changing, getting ready to accommodate him in the most intimate sense.

When he was finished with one side of her neck, he went to the other side to plunder there, also. Emma was nearly dizzy when he finally stopped to peel off her shirt. She hadn't even noticed he'd unbuttoned it. He smoothed it over her shoulders and down her arms, when it wouldn't go any further, he looked baffled for a moment and if she'd had the energy she might have laughed.

Zach looked down finally realizing he needed to pull it from her jeans and hissed. She'd worn sexy underwear. Just in case she did manage to get him naked. Apparently, he liked what he saw. His hands immediately went to caress her lace covered breasts. Her hands were trapped inside the shirt he'd forgotten all about. Smooth, he was not.

He made up for it with actions, kissed the tops of her breasts and then let his tongue dip below the fabric to tantalize her. He teased and kissed and licked until she was squirming for more.

"Zach, stop teasing."

He looked up at her with lust filled eyes. "Savoring every inch, not teasing."

"You've got a lot more inches to go, let's move this along, cowboy."

He grinned, "As you wish."

He unsnapped her bra, but it didn't go very far. He huffed out a breath. "Left you trapped, didn't I? Couldn't help myself, that lace covering your generous breasts, called to me and I had to answer."

He pulled the shirt out of her waistband and freed her hands, as he tossed the shirt on the couch. Then Zach sent her lace bra flying on top of the shirt and went straight back to enjoying her breasts. Clearly the man liked boobs. He ran his thumbs over her furled nipples and then lightly pinched them. She thought she might explode from the sensations he was stirring.

When he lowered his head and took one nipple in his mouth she nearly died from the exquisite pleasure. It was nothing at all like breast feeding a child. She'd heard people compare the two and right then and there decided they were idiots. Nothing compared to Zach's hot mouth suckling her. Nothing.

He gave both breasts equal attention and then that clever mouth started moving lower, kissing, licking and nibbling her torso until he met with her jeans.

He looked up with a sheepish grin. "Let's get the boots off first, so I don't trap you in your jeans like I did the shirt."

"Glad to see your brain still has some blood

left in it."

"Not much believe me. Sit on the couch so I can pull them off."

It would be easier for her to toe them off herself. But he seemed to be having such a good time she didn't want to disrupt him, besides the fact that her knees were pretty wobbly. She might just fall down into a heap. So, she did as directed, and sat on the couch.

Zach knelt at her feet and gently pulled her boot off the right foot. He rolled her sock down and slipped it off. She was shocked when he kissed her toes and the arch. She'd had no idea her feet were erogenous zones, but his gentle kisses were driving her wild. Even her ankle loved his attention.

When he'd kissed every inch of her right foot, he proceeded to do the same to the left one. She took the exquisite torture as long as she could. When he just wouldn't stop, she pushed him back with the other foot.

She panted out, "Zach, time to move it along cowboy. Let's get to the main event."

The man set her foot on the floor, grinned at her, stood, and pulled her up with him. He massaged her breasts and finally reached for her belt. Zach unbuckled the belt and drew it slowly through the loops, she pulled his head down for a steamy kiss as he unzipped her fly.

While he pushed her jeans down her legs, she held on to his shoulders to step out of them. Zach groaned when he saw her standing there in only her bright red lacy panties. He growled out, "Emma, you're trying to kill me."

"Just making sure I had your full attention."

"Darlin', you could be wearing a gunny sack and you'd still have my full attention."

"I'll remember that."

He took a good long look at her before he pulled her drenched panties down her legs and then stepped back for another good long look. She had to force herself not to squirm under his avid gaze.

"You're overdressed for this party, Zach."

He looked down at himself and then started pulling clothes off so fast he was a blur. While he was engaged, she pulled the condoms out of her jeans pocket. When he was naked, it was her turn, for a good long look.

"Mmm, so much better in the daylight."

Zach choked out a strangled chuckle. "So much better fully awake, too."

She smiled and then sashayed over to the steps for the bed and climbed up onto it. She looked back over her shoulder at the man standing stock still. "You going to join me or continue to play statue."

Shirley Penick

He sighed. "Just admiring the view, darlin'. It's a great view."

"Well, come admire it up close and personal, Zach."

∞∞∞

Zach didn't have to be told twice, he made it up onto the bed in one leap. Emma laughed at his antics. He'd wanted to keep up the worship of her very fine self, her legs and the paradise between them, but he didn't think he had any more control left. Since she wanted to move along, he decided he would save the rest of her to enjoy another time. Zach definitely wanted a taste of her, but he could wait, he could be very patient when he wanted to be.

They laid down on the bed and he resumed kissing her, her lips were addictive, he could kiss her for hours and not grow weary of it. She held his head in place as he explored every millimeter of her mouth, and let his hands roam over her body.

Emma gasped when he touched her most intimate spot, she was more than ready for him, but he wanted to give her pleasure before he took his own. In his experience a woman enjoyed love making more if she was working on her second orgasm rather than her first. He had no trouble with ensuring she would enjoy it all.

As his fingers set up a motion designed to drive her up and over that edge, he continued to give her deep drugging kisses. Her skin was very sensitive to his touch and it wasn't long before her body readied itself for release. He pushed one long finger into her tight, hot, wet channel and she flew with his name on her lips.

It was by far the best sound he'd ever heard in his whole life. He slowed his movements drawing her release out and gentling his touch.

Emma sighed and looked up through her lashes. "That was amazing, man-made orgasms are so much better."

He grinned, "The best is yet to come, my love."

He snagged the strip of condoms Emma had tossed on the bed and tore one open.

Her eyes lit up. "Oh, let me."

The pleasure was so intense, he nearly had a heart attack, as she slowly rolled the protection on his straining cock. He gritted his teeth and held on to his restraint for dear life as she took her time.

After what seemed like hours she said, "Okay, all done." Then she rolled onto her back and opened her legs in invitation.

He happily obliged the woman, taking care to go slow, to allow her body to stretch and take him in. She'd been tight on his finger, so he knew she needed a slow breach to become accustomed to his size.

When he was fully seated, she squirmed around a bit to make herself more comfortable, then arched her back and he slid in a little deeper. He waited a moment to make sure she was ready before he pulled back, so he could slide forward again.

After only a few thrusts, they found their rhythm and the ride began in earnest. She, whipping him to greater speed and force, they climbed the hills of ecstasy together. They rode higher and higher until they took wings and flew together up into the clouds of joy.

He shook his head wondering where all the poetry was coming from, he'd never thought of himself as a cowboy poet, but apparently, she brought it out in him.

Zach started to roll them to their sides, but Emma held on and murmured, "Just a minute or two longer, you feel so good plastered to me."

He propped himself up on his elbows and kissed her forehead and nose. She tilted her face, so he could reach her lips and he sunk into a warm, loving kiss. After a few moments of deep languorous kisses, she patted his ass and he figured that was his clue to move. He rolled them to their sides and their legs tangled together as they stayed close enough to touch and continue kissing.

When they stopped for air she whispered, "That was much better than the first time."

He chuckled, a low rumbling sound. "You think? I was awake and active this time."

"I had no idea how amazing it could be. Now I know what all the fuss is about."

"None of your other lovers gave you an inkling?"

She looked him in the eye. "You are my one and only lover, Zach. I've never been interested in doing that with anyone else."

Well hell, he was such a dumb ass. Fucking stupid beyond compare. "I'm so sorry. Emma. So damn sorry I left you alone all this time. Can you ever forgive me? Maybe even give me a do-over?"

She looked into his eyes again. "That's pretty much what I thought we were doing here, Zach."

His heart leaped with joy. A slow smile spread across his face until he could feel himself grinning. He watched as that same slow smile spread across her face and she was grinning back at him. Maybe, just maybe they could work this out. God, he hoped so. He made that thought into a prayer. God please help me to take the right steps, so Emma and I can be together, with Tony, as a real family.

Chapter 23

The rest of the time Tony was with his grandmother, Emma and Zach spent together in the trailer. They talked and made love. They cooked food on his little stove and then made love. They even talked a little about the future and what it might hold for them. Both of them decided they needed to work some things out if they wanted to proceed, so they tabled that discussion and made love instead.

When Zach got word his mom was leaving Mesa, they had one last time to enjoy each other. This time was different than all the rest, because they didn't know when they would be able to be together alone again. They made love slowly, savoring each touch, each kiss. Emma tried to memorize everything about Zach, to keep it close so she could pull the memory out whenever she wanted to or needed to.

She reveled in his groans and shivers and moans. She tried to kiss and lick every inch of his incredible body and he returned the favor, she wondered if he was trying to memorize her like she was him. She wanted to give him a memory that would last a lifetime, if need be. Not that she was going to give up on her dream of being by his side, but she wanted to make the most of this last time of closeness while in Arizona.

When they got back to Colorado, real life would settle in and they wouldn't have the freedom they had here. She would have to work, and he would need to get his body and his horses back in prime shape to start the competition round. Calving season would be in full swing and he would probably help out as much as he could with that too.

They might be able to have a rendezvous in his trailer once in a while, but it would be nothing compared to the freedom they had shared in Tucson. This place would forever hold a certain charm for her as the place that she and Zach had found each other once again.

When his mom texted that she was getting close, he and Emma straightened up the trailer and walked away. She hoped that they would be able to use it for a secret rendezvous at her family's ranch.

She mentioned that idea to Zach and his eyes lit up. "Absolutely. I'll probably stay in it while I'm at the Rockin' K rather than in the bunkhouse. You are welcome to join me any time."

They met his sister and her husband in the driveway. Natalie's face turned pink when she saw them. She said sheepishly, "So, you probably noticed we weren't around much."

Alex muttered, "At all."

Natalie nudged him with her elbow. "We don't get a lot of time together alone anymore. I hope you don't think badly of us for deserting you and spending all our time in one of the cabins. It's just..."

Emma looked at Zach and saw the same realization. Natalie and Alex had no idea they'd been holed up in the trailer the same amount of time. Emma felt relief at not having to confess where they had been. She'd not realized she was worried about explaining, until she didn't have to. She was also glad they had ranch hands that had taken care of the horses, not very responsible of them to indulge like they had.

Zach said, "No worries Nat, we managed to keep ourselves occupied."

Natalie asked, "You won't say anything to mom or the boys."

"Nope, your life is your own business, none of mine."

Then he winked at Emma and she beamed back at him.

Betty drove into the yard and parked the car. The boys all shimmied out of their seatbelts and charged their parents talking a mile a minute about how much fun they'd had on their journey. Betty got the boys' attention and said, "You three take your loot to your room and we'll all meet in the kitchen, so you can tell your parents all about your trip."

The three boys obediently gathered their belongings and trooped into the house.

Betty looked at the four adults, one at a time, a knowing perusal. Then she grinned at them and said, "Clearly the four of you had a very good time as well. Just as I'd hoped. Let's get inside, so the kids can talk *your* ear off for a change. I'm going to go sit in my room for a little while in the silence. The blessed, blessed silence."

Natalie and Alex followed Betty into the house.

Emma held back and whispered to Zach, "Did she mean what I think she meant?"

He grimaced. "Yeah, I think she did. Guess we look as relaxed as Nat and Alex."

Emma felt her face heat. "Oh."

Zach shrugged and tugged on her arm. "Come on, Tony will get antsy if we don't get in there. I think maybe I need to buy mom some flowers, or maybe even a new house, or send her on a vacation."

Emma giggled. "Maybe you should."

They walked together shoulder to shoulder into the noise and chaos of three little boys who'd had a grand adventure and wanted to relate every single detail to their parents. None of whom, complained in the least, to hearing all about it. They were, all four, quite relaxed, after all.

Emma marveled at how quickly her life had changed in a twenty-four-hour period. She and Zach were determined to find a way to make their little family work. She would have to work out some things, her job, and Tony's school were the top two. But she'd always believed where there was a will there was a way.

∞∞∞∞

Zach was thinking hard about the best way to arrange his season on the circuit, in order to both make the most money and compete where he needed to, and remain close enough to Colorado to see Emma and his son. Once Tony was out of school, Emma might be willing to come out on the circuit with him, if she could find a way to keep her business going.

He could probably support them both, but Emma was not about to sit around doing nothing and she was proud of her business. It was going strong and made her happy. There was certainly a way to work it all out. It was just going to take some thinking and doing on both their parts.

Zach sensed she was as committed to finding a way as he was, so there had to be a solution. They just needed to find it. Probably easier said than done, but no one ever said life was easy. Most of the best things in life came from hard work and determination to succeed. They both had a lot of those characteristics, so they would eventually figure it out.

He decided to spend the last day, before they left, on a family outing on the horses. He had two that got antsy on long drives, so taking them out for the day would help prepare them for the journey. He'd talked to Alex about using one of the kids' horses for Tony, Alex had suggested the pony that Vern rode. Wes had graduated to a gentle mare, but Vern wasn't quite ready yet.

Zach had mentioned the idea to Emma and she'd agreed that it would be fun to take a ride, and assured him that Tony was quite capable as a rider. He packed some sandwiches, chips, fruit, and cookies into a saddle bag with drinks in the other side.

The horses were saddled and ready to go. He'd need to adjust stirrups, but then they could be on their way.

Tony came into the kitchen with his customary exuberance. He was dressed exactly right for a ride. "Mama said we were going riding! I love riding, but it's hard to go during school."

"Yes, what good is a mini-vacation without having a horse ride?"

Tony hugged Zach's knees. "Yay, thanks, Daddy."

Zach's heart melted every single time Tony called him daddy. It was quickly becoming his favorite word. He cleared his throat. "Gotta get my ponies ready for their long ride back to your house. Figured we could have some fun while we do it."

"Am I going to ride one of your horses?" Tony asked with wide eyes.

"No, you're going to ride Vern's pony. Your mom and I are going to ride my horses."

Tony nodded and hopped from foot to foot. "How soon are we going?"

"As soon as your mom is ready, we'll head out. I was just finishing up packing us a lunch."

Emma sailed into the room looking like the most beautiful horsewoman Zach had ever seen. His mouth watered with the desire to pull her close and kiss her. Not having the freedom to do that was driving him a little crazy. But she wanted to wait until they had things figured out before letting Tony in on anything.

Zach knew that was wise, because the kid was going to have a million questions, so they needed to know how they were going to answer those questions first. But it was still damn difficult not to pull her into his arms and kiss the stuffing out of her. He settled for a long look and a wink that made her cheeks turn a little pink, and then he grabbed up the saddle bags and led his family out to the horses.

Zach laid the saddle bag on the horse he was riding and lifted Tony into the saddle of his pony for the day. He'd guessed pretty close on the stirrup length but still needed to adjust them one notch. By the time he was finished he noticed Emma had already adjusted her own. Zach untied the pony and handed Tony the reins, then climbed on his own horse and they walked the horses out of the yard.

They had Tony between them. Emma asked her son, "Doing good, Tony?"

"Yes, Mama, this is a very nice horse. What's his name, Daddy?"

"His name is Paint, for the splotches."

"Nice name." Tony reached forward and patted the pony on the neck. "You're a good horse, Paint, and we'll have fun on our ride today."

The horse nodded his head in agreement.

Once they got out further into the field, Tony asked, "Can we go a little faster now?"

Zach chuckled and glanced at Emma who nodded. "Sure thing, Son, need to give these guys some exercise."

Zach led the horses into a trot. He wanted to make sure Tony could handle the faster pace. But he seemed to be doing fine and had an enormous smile on his face. Zach couldn't blame him. It was a mild, pretty day, and they were riding through an open field on a family adventure. He couldn't think of a better way to spend the day.

Once Tony was completely comfortable the questions started.

"Why is there no grass?"

"This is a desert, Son, it's too dry for grass."

"Everyone says we live in an alpine desert, but we still have some grass. All there is here is pokey bushes."

"Yeah, but that's because you're in the mountains and the snow waters the grass and so does the rain. They don't get snow here and not a lot of rain either."

"Is that why there are really big cactus plants? We have little ones but not huge like these."

"That's exactly why. There are some grasses in different places, some like you're used to, others that might look like weeds, but the cattle still like to eat them. The cattle have to go further to find enough food."

Tony nodded solemnly. "Are there any different critters we don't have in Colorado?"

The kid was testing his knowledge. He shook his head. "Not so much. But you've got critters they don't have here. Like moose and elk, they need more wetness and greener grasses. Although they might get a roadrunner occasionally."

"Like on the cartoon?"

Zach couldn't hold back his smile. "Yep, they live in the desert, but usually down a bit further south into Mexico."

"It would be fun to see one."

"It would be."

Tony fell silent after that and Zach breathed a sigh of relief, he wasn't an expert on the flora and fauna of Arizona by any stretch of the imagination. The kid needed a good set of encyclopedias. Did they even sell those anymore?

It was easier to search for things now, but you had to know what you were looking for. Tony probably wasn't old enough to use a search engine, he would have to know how to spell. With an encyclopedia you could turn pages and look at pictures on everything. It seemed like some things were lost in the modern age of technology.

Tony asked, "Where are we going to picnic? I'm getting a little hungry and thirsty."

Emma rolled her eyes; it was not quite noon and Zach was certain Tony had eaten a good breakfast. But he didn't mind stopping.

"See those big rocks up ahead? I thought we would go up on them and check out the view."

"Yay. Can we go faster?"

Emma said, "Tony, you don't want to wear out your pony, he's got short legs."

"We can try and if he gets tired, we can stop." The pony shook his head like he was all in. "See even Paint thinks it's a good idea."

Zach chuckled. "We can try it, but if your horse starts to slow down, let him. Okay?"

"Yes, sir."

Zach pushed his horse into a canter and the pony leapt to keep up. When they got to the rocks Zach slowed his horse to a walk and the others did, too. The pony and Tony had done just fine on the short canter across the remaining area.

Zach said, "We'll have to go single file up the path to the top of the rocks. Emma, you go first, then Tony and I'll bring up the rear. Watch for rattlers and steer clear of them. This is their home, we're the trespassers here. But that doesn't mean I won't shoot one if I need to."

Chapter 24

E mma was relieved they didn't run into any snakes. She could certainly handle herself around them and Tony had been taught precaution, but not having to deal with them was far better. The view from atop the rocks was lovely, it looked out over a valley with some mountains not too far in the distance.

She wasn't sure what mountain range it was, but she didn't want to ask and have Tony start up another round of twenty questions. She didn't know how much Zach actually knew about the area. He'd lived most of his life in Colorado and then had been on the road ever since, he probably had a little knowledge of a lot of places but not a tremendous amount of anywhere in particular. Except maybe Colorado and Tony had already peppered everyone in the house with questions about that.

They had a pleasant lunch and they let Tony ramble on about whatever came into his head.

"I heard Gramma B tell Aunty F that she had come to visit to give the parents of the boys time to figure some things out. What did you have to figure out?"

Emma choked on the mouthful of water she'd just taken a drink of and looked over to see Zach with a deer in headlights look.

Tony didn't let them answer but continued on, "She told Aunty F that another grandchild or two would be nice and she said I needed a sibling. Is that like a brother or sister? Are you two going to start kissing?"

Oh, good lord, they weren't ready to answer questions like that. She decided to hedge. "What would you think about that idea?"

"I might like it if Daddy got to be around more. Cindy said her mommy and daddy sleep in the same bed. But Daddy is sleeping in the bunk house. Cindy said her daddy only slept on the couch sometimes and that was when her mommy was really mad at her dad. Are you mad at Daddy?"

Dammit this was getting worse by the minute. She looked at Zach to try to gauge which way to take this discussion.

He shrugged. "Tony, I'm staying in the bunk house because I haven't seen your mom in a long time, and we need to get to know each other better. You know your mom and I aren't married right? Well usually people get married before they sleep in the same bed."

Tony laughed. "No Daddy, that's silly. All my uncles slept in the same bed with their girlfriends before they got married."

Zach clearly had nothing to say to that statement. So, Emma took the conversational ball. "Not at first, they didn't, Tony. Zach's only been here a couple of weeks."

That answer seemed to satisfy the boy and Emma breathed a sigh of relief.

A good ten minutes later, Tony said, "If you do want to kiss and have a baby, I suppose that would be okay, it's been kinda fun here to have kids to play with all the time, even if they are stinky to start with."

Neither she nor Zach said a word.

Zach wasn't going to touch that statement with a ten-foot pole. It would be like trying to stroll through a mine field or walk barefoot over the jagged sharp a'a lava he'd heard one of the Paniolo from Hawaii talk about. Apparently, some of the lava flows were liquid enough and cooled to a smooth texture but the a'a lava flow could cut a person to ribbons. The Hawaiian Cowboy had said even in boots it was dangerous and they had to make sure the cattle were kept safe from those fields.

That's pretty much exactly how he felt about Tony's comment, one false move and he could be cut and bleeding. Since Emma's mouth was clamped tight, he gathered she was feeling the same way. He needed to think about another subject to distract Tony, like right now.

He couldn't think of a thing. Maybe horses. Maybe get Tony talking about his own horse. "What's the name of your horse, Tony?"

"My pony is named Butternut, which is kind of a girly name so maybe if you do decide to have a baby you should get a girl, so she can ride Butternut and I can move onto a bigger horse. I am five years old; Wes has a bigger horse."

Emma said, "Wes is two years older than you."

"I know mama, but I'm a really good horse rider. And Butternut is so slow, not nearly as fast as Paint is."

Zach needed to change the subject and quickly before this turned into a full-fledged war over his horse's size. Tony's face had taken on a defiant expression and Emma looked equally firm in her convictions. He didn't want Tony to remonstrate to his mother, over something that wasn't about to change, at least not any time soon. Zach agreed with Emma; Tony was still a little small for a mare. Another two years of growth would be about right.

"Have you tried roping from your pony?"

Tony couldn't resist the lure of that question, thank God. He turned to Zach, "Just once, Butternut did a good job standing still, while I practiced with Uncle Cade. I missed more than I hit though, so I need to practice more."

"That's a good reason to keep Butternut a little longer, you're closer to the calf on Butternut than you would be on a larger mare. I think that you need to be able to hit your target every time on Butternut before you move onto a larger horse."

Zach could see Tony thinking that over. "I would rather have a bigger horse, but it would be easier to practice roping on Butternut."

Zach let out the breath he'd been holding, and Emma gave him a thumbs up behind Tony's back. Score one for the dad. Zach nodded seriously. "Yep, it's best to learn roping one step at a time. That way you become an expert instead of some guy who is just average."

"Are you an expert, Daddy?"

"I'm close to that in a couple of events, good in a few more and just average in a couple. But that's pretty normal. To be an all-around cowboy it's better to focus on your two best events, and work on those, to perfect them, rather than mucking around with all the others. It took me a year or two to decide which ones I was best at and liked the most."

"What two events do you do?" Tony asked, his head cocked to one side as if he was trying to guess.

"Tie-down roping and team roping."

Tony nodded sagely. "I like the roping events, too. But some of those bucking broncos and bulls get to be crazy. It's fun to watch."

"It is fun, but it can be dangerous, those are some mighty cranky critters."

"Did you ride some cranky critters? Do you have any scars from rodeoing?"

"Yes, and I have a couple of scars." Zach nodded; it was all part of the sport. No scars meant you weren't trying very hard.

"Can I see them?"

"Not now, the next time we shower I can show you."

"Yay!"

Zach asked, "Are we ready to ride back to the house?"

Tony nodded, and Emma got to her feet. They'd pretty much polished off the lunch. There were only empty water bottles and trash left.

Tony gathered that up to put in a bag Zach had brought. Zach and Emma shook out the blanket and rolled it up to tie behind his saddle.

Zach put Tony up on his pony and the boy turned the horse toward the path they'd come up. Emma sighed and caught up with her son. Tony was fearless, he did not seem to have a timid bone in his body. Timorous was not something that Tony knew anything about.

He'd obviously been surrounded by family that let him learn and grow without the smothering he'd heard some single mothers leaned toward. Of course, Emma being the only female sibling probably had something to do with that. She and Meg had to hold their own against seven men, not counting the ranch hands. It was evening out now with all her brothers getting married.

By the time they reached the single file part of the path Tony had talked Emma into letting him lead the way. Zach figured it was safe enough, so he took the rear. He could still keep an eye on everything, which is probably why Emma had consented, so she could keep an eye on Tony also.

Zach was proud to see his son didn't rush the pony but allowed the animal to choose its own speed. Tony was a good kid, still only five, but a good kid. He wanted to be in on shaping that young mind and growing personality.

Chapter 25

Tony was thrilled with the plan to sleep in the trailer on the way back to Colorado. Emma thought he might explode with enthusiasm. She'd had to show him every little bit of it. Which she'd done while Zach had loaded his horses. Once Tony's curiosity had been assuaged and the horses were loaded there were many good-byes and promises to be back soon to visit.

Tony had invited his cousins, aunt and uncle, and Grammy to come to Colorado to meet the rest of his family. Emma had been a little surprised by his hospitality, but then realized he'd never seen anything different, so she supposed it made sense.

They loaded up into the truck and waved a final goodbye as they set their sights on Colorado.

"Mama, am I going to go to school next week?"

"Yes, Tony we should get back in time for you to go on Monday, or Tuesday at the latest."

"Good, we are having an eye doctor come to our class on Wednesday."

"I didn't know that. But I guess you have been studying the parts of the body."

"Yeah. I think the eye part is the best. Teacher told us all about what an eye doctor does. But he's not going to do all that, we're just going to look at the Smelling Chart. It has letters that get smaller and smaller toward the bottom."

Zach chuckled. "I think it's called a Snellen chart, Tony. S-n-e-l-l-e-n, smelling is s-m-e-l-l-i-n-g. Snellen is the name of the man that invented it."

Tony laughed. "That's good, I was wondering about its name. I wondered if we had to smell it, or if it was stinky or something. Snellen is better. If I invented it, we could call it the Tony chart, or maybe the Kipling chart."

Emma saw Zach frown and wondered what he was thinking. If she and Zach actually did manage to work things out and stay together, they would need to think about getting Tony's name changed to his father's name, especially if she and Zach got married. And wasn't that putting the cart before the horse? There was a lot to work out before they got to that point.

When she got home, she was going to make a list of all the things that would have to be sorted out in order for her and Zach to have even the ghost of a chance. She wasn't going to give up the hope that they could make it happen. She had loved the boy from afar, now she knew she loved the man up close and personal.

This might be a good thing to talk to her mom about, or maybe her dad. She chuckled to herself, probably Grandpa K would be the best source for firm advice.

She wasn't quite certain what kind of sleeping arrangements there would be for the next two nights. Probably her and Tony in the queen-sized bed and Zach on the fold-out couch. She was glad she felt comfortable around Zach now, it would have been awkward, before they'd had their marathon sex day, to travel with him and sleep in the same room. But it wasn't a big deal now.

Although they would have to be careful around Tony, so he didn't get any more ideas than the ones he already had. She internally shook her head at her son and the conversations he had with Cindy. She didn't know whether to say something about it or not. Probably best to leave it alone. Cindy had a new sibling and it was probably just her way of processing that.

Tony piped up from the backseat, "Can we play 'I spy with my little eye'?"

Emma smiled at her son. "Sure, Tony, you start."

They played I Spy for over an hour before Tony couldn't find anything else to spy, the drive had turned monotonous as they left the cities behind and hit the open road. He went back to entertaining himself with all the things Zach had bought for him. Zach's mom had added a few things too, but she'd mostly bought him clothes. Emma couldn't argue with that, Tony was growing like a weed and keeping him in clothes that weren't too short or tight was a challenge.

It had been an excellent visit all the way around. Zach's family had been so warm and open with both her and Tony. She'd been a little worried that they would blame her for not finding a way to tell Zach about his son. Fortunately, her fears had been ungrounded, and they'd welcomed both of them into the family.

Zach drove in relative silence once they'd stopped playing the game with Tony. Emma seemed to be content thinking her own thoughts. Zach was glad of that because he was brooding about what Tony had said about being a Kipling. He wanted Tony to have his last name. Tony was his son and he was proud of that fact; he wanted the world to know.

He needed to ask Emma if she would be willing to give Tony his name. Of course, he was still thinking about getting Emma to change her name to his, too. There was getting to be quite a few things he wanted to talk to her about.

Zach didn't think it would be a good idea to do that in the truck with Tony in the back seat, even if he was napping, he might wake up and the things they needed to talk about had to be decided, before they mentioned them to Tony. Maybe he should make a list and secure a time to talk, like an appointment almost. After they got Tony on the school bus might be a good time. It would probably take several hours, so maybe one hour each morning for a week or so.

He also needed to get his butt in the practice ring with a calf or two. Maybe he should just join the rest of the hands as the birthing time was gearing up. There was roping to be done there aplenty. Although it wasn't quite the same as competition roping, where the calf was basically directed in a straight line. But the real roping that was done on a ranch was certainly the precursor to what the events had become. It might be good for him to work with some more variables.

Zach needed to get back on his exercise program also, he needed to keep his body in shape. He'd not completely laid off of that, but he wasn't being as diligent as he normally would be.

He nearly sighed, but he didn't want Emma to question him. There was a lot to be done in the next few weeks before he got back on the circuit.

He'd have to make sure he was doing all he needed to, so something didn't sneak up on him.

To get Emma's attention, he cleared his throat. "I think we need to set up some time to talk about things. Maybe at the start of the day, once Tony is on his way to school."

Emma looked at him for a few moments and then slowly nodded. "I could do that. I'm going to need to catch up with my clients when we get back, but your suggestion is a good one. There is a lot to talk about."

"I do appreciate you and Tony coming with me. I know my family was thrilled to have you."

"They were great. I wasn't sure if they'd be —" she glanced back at Tony and relaxed, "—less welcoming. Maybe a little angry about things."

"It was probably good I gave them a heads up, so they could think things through." He nodded his head back toward Tony.

"Watching a movie, I think. Headphones anyway."

Zach nodded. "Probably that new one mom bought. You don't mind her spoiling him a little, do you?"

"No. I think he'll be fine. He's an only child so he hasn't had to share with anyone. Plus, she mostly bought clothes... you on the other hand..."

He laughed. "Guilty. I've never bought

clothes for a kid. Toys are easy, clothes are hard. I went with easy."

"Yeah, but you did a good job on the assortment, not all just electronics. I think he's played with everything."

"Thanks. I've seen some of the other parents on the circuit and noticed what they had in their kids' road trip entertainment kits."

Emma asked, "Are there a lot of kids traveling?"

"More than I expected. They sometimes do a home-schooling group if we're at a rodeo location for a few days."

"Really? I never would have guessed."

Zach shrugged. "Yeah, it's a sport that is year-round, so unless the kids stay home, they need to be taught, and with the co-op thing it helps spread the teaching around. That way the kids aren't only by themselves with their parents. It gives them socialization and also teaches them to learn under different adults."

"How come you know all this?"

He glanced at her with a mischievous look. "I've got a couple of friends that have their kids with them, we got to shooting the shit one day, and that was the shit we were shooting."

Emma rolled her eyes at him and he grinned unrepentantly. "It's kind of valuable information in this instance."

He sobered and caught her eye for a moment before turning back to the road. "Yes, it is, quite valuable."

God, he hoped they could work out a way for her and Tony to join him on the road. His eyes had been opened to what life with her and Tony could be like and he liked it, he liked it a lot.

Emma had lapsed into silence and he hoped she was thinking about what he'd revealed and what it could mean to the both of them.

Chapter 26

The drive back was relatively uneventful. Tony loved 'camping' in the trailer. Emma had wondered if he would complain about not going to hotels for the swimming pool, but he didn't even mention it. He loved helping Zach set up the portable corrals, Zach probably could have done it quicker without Tony's help, but he didn't let on that that was the case.

Zach really was a good father.

The drive had been a lot quieter, especially when Tony was asleep. She and Zach had more to talk about than ever, but they kept relatively silent about all those things. She supposed it was so Tony didn't hear them and start demanding answers. Emma wanted to demand answers. What was Zach thinking? Did he just want to come visit his son when he got the chance? She didn't think so.

Was he thinking they could just join him in the summer and on school vacations? The conversation about the home schooling indicated he was thinking about having them along with him during the school year.

She had no idea how Tony would react to that, he loved school. He could easily learn as much on the road as he did in a formal environment. Emma was good at math and science and Zach was good at geography and history. They both were readers. She'd seen a stack of books in one of the closets in his trailer and she'd seen him reading on his phone the first night in the hotel, when she went over to ask him about something. So, she decided that between the two of them they could easily handle grade school.

Middle school and high school might be a bigger challenge, but that wouldn't be an issue for a good five or six years. So, school would be fine.

If she got all her clients' books on the cloud, she could easily work on them remotely. She might be able to pick up some other clients while on the road, there was a lot of bookkeeping involved in rodeo and a good accountant might be valuable. So, her business would also be fine. It would take some hard work over the next couple of months, but she thought it was doable.

What she was the least sure of was her relationship with Zach. They'd had great sex, and she knew he'd loved her in the past, but he'd not said a word about loving her now. She'd not said anything either. He'd kind of hinted at it, but she needed to know for sure. Did he want them to get married? Have more children, or was he just getting close to her, so he could see his son?

She vowed to herself that the question of love and marriage needed to be the first thing they talked about, when they started to have what she was thinking of, as negotiation meetings. Emma wasn't going to completely uproot her life without a full commitment from Zach. Old fashioned, maybe, but that's the way she was built.

Emma had not had a chance to talk to her elders yet for advice. Tony had monopolized their time since the moment they'd driven in the driveway. Telling everyone all about how much fun they'd had on the trip. As Emma had predicted the café had been one of the highlights, but the swimming pools and helping Zach with the portable corrals had been right up there. He'd talked nonstop until bedtime and then had fallen sound asleep. By then Emma and everyone else was exhausted so they'd all headed for bed, too.

Now it was time to get Tony to the bus and then she and Zach were going to have their first meeting. She was working hard to keep the nerves at bay. This was Zach, the man she'd just spent ten days with. They had been wonderful days, when Tony had talked non-stop telling her family every little detail of the trip, he'd had insights and joy about things she hadn't even noticed, and that had helped her remember all the fun they had enjoyed.

Zach met her and Tony in the yard.

"Daddy, daddy I'm going to school today and tell all my friends how much fun we had while we were gone. Mama filled up my backpack with the homework and books for the library. It's library day today, so I get to get new ones. Cindy will be happy to have me back and I have so much to tell her."

Zach laughed at Tony's enthusiasm, which sent a thrill through Emma. She loved Zach's joy in his son, her little guy certainly embraced life. Zach knelt down to give Tony a hug and said, "I hope you have a great day at school."

"Oh, I will! Are your horses happy here?"

"They are very happy, munching on grass."

Tony frowned. "I hope they don't get cold. It's warmer in Arizona than it is here."

"They'll be fine, don't worry."

"Okay." Tony skipped down the drive toward the road and Emma and Zach trailed him. Emma glanced at Zach and noticed he was a little stiff. Was he nervous too?

She gave him a small smile and he returned a lopsided one. Yep, it looked like he was nervous too, which made her feel better. So, she reached for his hand and squeezed it. He clung, and that made her feel even better. Zach took a deep breath and a genuine smile curved his lips. When they got near the street, they dropped hands by silent mutual consent, they needed to work out their relationship before they broadcast it to the world.

∞∞∞

Zach hugged his son and watched him climb aboard the school bus. Tony waved and then was lost among the kids. He turned to Emma and they started back along the drive to the house.

"Do you want to take some horses out for our meeting? Maybe ride out to your land. I haven't seen all the construction."

He detected Emma relaxing at that idea, she looked as tense as he was feeling. Maybe getting out on the horses for a little while would calm them both down. "Yes, I'm not going to start working with my clients until this afternoon, so I have time. I'll need to get my boots."

"I'll saddle the horses while you do that."

She gave him a sweet smile. "Perfect. I'll grab us some drinks too. Saddle Chika for me, I haven't taken her out for a while."

"Will do."

They were ready to ride out quickly and Zach drew a deep breath of the morning air. It was chilly, but dry, with blue skies and no clouds. The ground was dry, too. They probably needed snow, but weren't likely to get it today so he and Emma would enjoy it while it lasted.

Emma kept up a running conversation as they rode past all her siblings' new homes. There were some finishing touches being made to Chase and Cade's houses, but they'd moved in. Landscaping would have to wait until the ground wasn't frozen. Zach enjoyed seeing the different structures each of them had decided on.

Beau and Alyssa's house came first. They had a nice big house that had an attached clinic that was nearly as large as the house. Zach wondered how many animals they could have in their veterinary clinic at one time, but it looked to him like it would hold quite a few.

Adam and Rachels home was built above the garage to give them a better view. They had huge windows that looked out toward the mountains on one side and the river on the other. Rachel being a photographer, and therefore an artist, had certainly put her stamp on the house.

Cade's house had a huge gymnasium, built above a full-sized swimming pool. There was no question Summer intended to keep her athlete's body in prime condition. Zach had noticed that Cade had slimmed down and was more muscle than he had been.

Chase and Katie's house was plenty large

enough for a family but had nothing extra built on, so it looked small in comparison. Only Emma and Drew hadn't built on their land and were still living in the family home. Drew's land was out past Emma's because he wanted to be the one closest to the road in case he was needed at the Sheriff's department.

They stopped at Emma's land and let the horses graze. Zach spread some blankets on the grass to keep the cold ground from chilling them and they sat down to talk.

He rubbed his hands on his thighs. Shit, he was about to make a fool of himself, but he just didn't have it in him to beat around the bush. "I don't know where to start exactly, so I'm just going to blurt it out. I love you and I love Tony and I want us to be a family. You may not be ready to hear that, and if you aren't, I'll wait as long as you need. But I want you to be fully aware, that I am not going to give up, until I have my ring on your finger and both you and Tony have my last name."

He shut his mouth and met her eyes. She gave him no indication how she felt about what he'd said, except her mouth was hanging open and there was a shocked look in her eyes.

Before she could say anything, he rushed on. "I don't know how we can work it all out, but I don't want to leave you and Tony behind in May. I want you to come with me. We can homeschool

Tony and he can join the co-ops that travel to the various rodeos. I don't know what to do about your business, I know it's impor—"

His words were cut off by a flying female landing in his lap and knocking him backward onto the blanket. Their hats had flown off and she'd grabbed his ears and was planting kisses all over his face. Now it was his turn to be flabbergasted except he didn't have time, because he was doing all he could to keep up with Emma.

Her mouth finally locked on his and she gave him the hottest, most erotic kiss of his entire life. She'd put her everything into it and his wits were whirling. When he realized some of the whirling was really lack of oxygen, he rolled them to their sides and pulled his mouth from hers.

He panted for a few moments and then managed to say, "Emma, sweetheart, not that I don't appreciate the enthusiasm, but breathing is a good thing too."

She grinned up at him, still panting herself.

"I take it you're onboard with the whole family idea?"

She tried to frown but it didn't quite get there. "Well it was a ham-handed proposal as those things go, but yes I'm very much on board."

"And the logistics, like your business?"

She put her hand over his mouth. "Don't you

worry about that. It will take some long hours the next few weeks, but I already have it all worked out."

She already had it worked out? So, she'd been thinking about it too. That gave him a great deal of peace and satisfaction. "So, you'll marry me?"

"Yes. But I'm not going out on the road until it's a done deal."

He raised his eyebrows. "In that case we need to get a move on."

"Yes. But I don't want big and fancy. Just my family and your family, here at the house."

"Are you sure about that? You've taken a lot of grief over me being absent, are you sure you don't want to... I don't know, rub it in their faces?"

"Nope, I want to marry you, surrounded by the people that stood beside me every day. Those are the only ones that matter."

"Fair enough. I better let my mom and sister know. I'm guessing mom will want to come early. Do you have a date in mind?"

She laughed. "You're going to think it's silly, but I think it's appropriate. Mother's Day."

He grinned at this woman he loved. "I think it's perfect. So, for our anniversary do you want to use the actual date or Mother's Day?"

"Both."

He laughed and pulled her to him to kiss her. The perfect way to seal the deal.

Epilogue

Zach McCoy was once again standing next to Drew in front of a group of people dressed in ultra-fancy duds. He was once again antici-pating the arrival of a small boy holding a pillow with rings tied on top.

Far from dreading the experience he could hardly wait for the event to happen. He glanced at the clock and stifled a groan. Was the damn thing even working? He was sure it had said the same time for a good twenty minutes.

He wasn't in an ill-fitting tux this time, but a tailor-made western suit of dark charcoal gray that fit him to perfection. He also wasn't in a church, but instead was in the main room of the house that had been his second home for nearly two decades.

Trying to distract himself, from the seconds moving so darn slowly, he thought over the last ten weeks. Every single one of those days had been glorious. He and Emma had worked hard. She with getting her clients' books onto the cloud. They'd tested his hotspot to make certain it would be adequate for her to use in their travels.

He'd worked out to get into the best shape of his life. And he'd practiced roping nearly every calf on the ranch. He was certain they all hid now when they saw him coming.

He and Emma had also worked at team roping. Her rope was hot. But her horse and she herself, had needed to work on the other aspects of the sport. Getting the calf to turn, then once Zach had caught the heels, turning Emma's horse to line up facing him, and then release the tension on the rope to let the calf go free. The two of them were shaping up to be a good team. They might not win this year, but with some practice they would in the future.

Tony had come home gloomy one day after school to announce that Cindy wasn't going to be attending his school anymore. When they'd questioned him about that, he'd related that Cindy's father had taken a position with the Pro Rodeo Cowboys Association and Cindy would be traveling with him, her baby brother, and her mom to rodeos.

She and Zach had assured Tony that he would see Cindy since there would certainly be times when they were all at the same rodeo. They'd not gone into great detail about what their lives were going to be like before, because they'd been concerned about Tony's reaction to not going to school. Once they explained that Tony would be doing the same as Cindy, he'd gotten excited. They'd been careful to remind Tony that he would not see Cindy every day, but they should see her at least occasionally.

Emma and he had managed to find time to sneak away to his trailer for some loving. Not as often as they both would have liked, but enough to keep them from going crazy. So, he'd had a fine ten weeks and if they could just get this show on the road, he would be able to relax.

Finally, the music changed, and Tony appeared in the doorway with his pillow. He'd not had one single complaint about being the ring bearer one more time, if it meant keeping his dad by his side, and he'd even consented to changing his last name to Zach's.

Tony had a huge smile on his face as he walked past his family members and right up to his father. Zach looked up from his son to see Lily gliding down the aisle, they'd decided on one attendant only for their small home wedding. And since Drew was his, it made sense to have Lily be hers.

Eight long seconds after Lily had reached the front, Zach finally saw his magnificent bride and her father appear. The breath whooshed out of him and his knees got weak at the sight before him. Emma was stunning. Her dress was a shiny white material that caressed her curves and nearly glowed, there were little sparkles on the neckline and around the hem. Her hair was up in a riot of curls with a long lace veil trailing down her back. She wore the diamond earrings and necklace he'd bought her as soon as she'd consented to be his wife.

She smiled up at him and Drew reached over to shut his mouth, so he didn't drool. He would have thanked Drew for being a great wing-man, but Zach couldn't take his focus off Emma, not for one second. He managed to remember to take the one step forward he was allowed to take and reached for her hand.

The rest of the ceremony was a blur, he was so focused on Emma. He did manage to repeat his vows in a strong clear voice. He didn't want anyone doubting he wasn't one hundred and ten percent on board with this marriage.

When the minister pronounced them man and wife, Zach was more than ready to kiss his bride, and Drew only had to tap him on the shoulder two or three times, before he let her lips go from his.

He nearly cheered when the pastor introduced them as Mr. and Mrs. Zach McCoy, instead he lifted Emma and twirled her in a circle while she laughed, and the guests joined in the merriment.

Zach managed to sit through the food and toasts and dancing. She threw her bouquet and he tossed out her garter. They were showered with bird seed and finally managed to escape the family and well-wishers.

Emma snuggled close to him and sighed. "It's done."

Zach kissed the top of her head. "It is, and I am so damn elated that you are my wife. I've been waiting for this day for many, many, years." He pulled her tight and felt contentment slide through him.

She laid her head on his shoulder. "Me too, we finally got our dream."

"We did and I'm not letting it go. I'm in this forever, Emma. I love you and I'm keeping you."

"Good, because I love you too, Zach, and I'm keeping you."

Drew pulled up in front of cabin one and said, "Your honeymoon awaits."

Zach grinned at her and opened the door to the vehicle. He got out and turned to give her his hand. Once she was on her feet, he picked her up over his shoulder and nudged the door closed, waived to Lily and Drew and carried his wife into the cabin they would be spending the week in. The week that would start the rest of their lives as husband and wife.

The End

If you enjoyed this story, please leave a review on Amazon, Bookbub, or Goodreads.

Thanks so much!

Also, by Shirley Penick

LAKE CHELAN SERIES

The Rancher's Lady: A Lake Chelan novella

Hank and Ellen's story

Sawdust and Satin: Lake Chelan #1

Chris and Barbara's story

Designs on Her: Lake Chelan #2

Nolan and Kristen's story

Smokin': Lake Chelan #3

Jeremy and Amber's story

Fire on the Mountain: Lake Chelan #4

Trey and Mary Ann's story

The Fire Chief's Desire: Lake Chelan #5

Greg and Sandy's story

Mysterious Ways: Lake Chelan #6

Scott and Nicole's story

BURLAP AND BARBED WIRE SERIES

A Cowboy for Alyssa: Burlap and Barbed Wire #1

Beau and Alyssa's story

Taming Adam: Burlap and Barbed Wire #2

Adam and Rachel's story

Tempting Chase: Burlap and Barbed Wire #3

Chase and Katie's story

Roping Cade: Burlap and Barbed Wire #4

Cade and Summer's story

Trusting Drew: Burlap and Barbed Wire #5

Drew and Lily's story

Emma's Rodeo Cowboy: Burlap and Barbed Wire #6

Emma and Zach's story

HELLUVA ENGINEER SERIES

Helluva Engineer

Steve and Patsy's story

About Shirley

What does a geeky math nerd know about writing romance?

That's a darn good question. As a former techy I've done everything from computer programming to international trainer. Prior to college I had lots of different jobs and activities that were so diverse, I was an anomaly.

None of that qualifies me for writing novels. But I have some darn good stories to tell and a lot of imagination.

I have lived in Colorado, Hawaii and currently reside in Washington. Going from two states with 340 days of sun to a state with 340 days of clouds, I had to do something to perk me up. And that's when I started this new adventure called author. Joining the Romance Writers of America and two local chapters, helped me learn the craft quickly and has been a ton of fun.

My family consists of two grown children, their spouses, two adorable grand-daughters, and one grand dog. My favorite activity is playing with my grand-daughters!

When the girls can't play with their amazing grandmother, my interests are reading and writing, yay! I started reading at a young age with the Nancy Drew mysteries and have continued to be an avid reader my whole life. My favorite reading material is romance, but occasionally if other stories creep into my to-be-read pile, I don't kick them out.

Some of the strange jobs I have held are a carnation grower's worker, a trap club puller, a pizza hut waitress, a software engineer, an international trainer, and a business program manager. I took welding, drafting and upholstery in high school, a long time ago, when girls didn't take those classes, so I have an eclectic bunch of knowledge and experience.

And for something really unusual... I once had a raccoon as a pet.

Join with me as I tell my stories, weaving real tidbits from my life in with imaginary ones. You'll have to guess which is which. It will be a hoot!

CPSIA information can be obtained
at www.ICGtesting.com
Printed in the USA
FSHW011951240719
60375FS

9 781077 295926